Date Due

DEC 7 '70			
12/10/70			
MAR 4 '71			
JUL 22 '71			

Demco 38-297

SOUTH TOWN

BY LORENZ GRAHAM

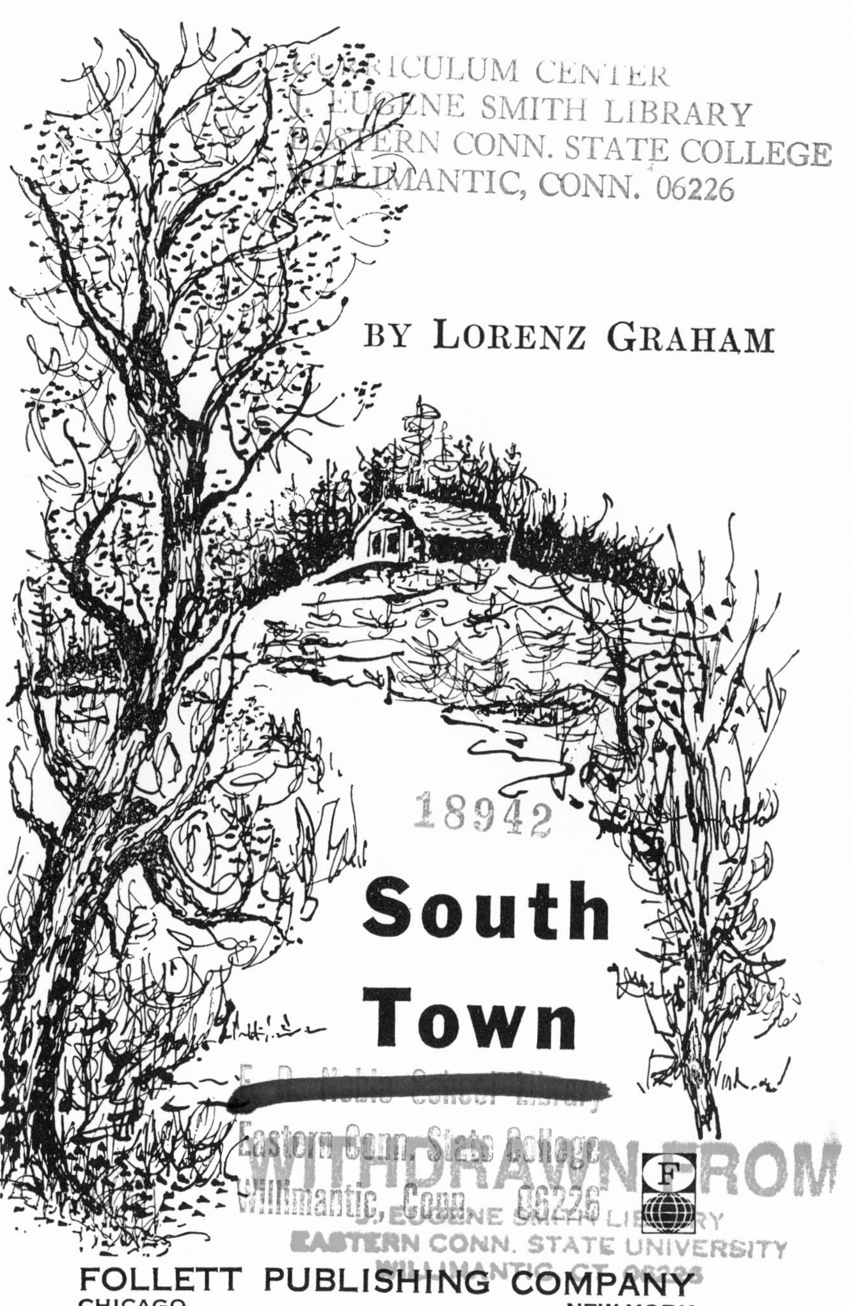

South Town

FOLLETT PUBLISHING COMPANY
CHICAGO NEW YORK

The Charles W. Follett Award

J

FOR

WORTHY CONTRIBUTIONS TO CHILDREN'S LITERATURE

Johnny Texas	*by Carol Hoff*	*1950*
All-of-a-Kind Family	*by Sydney Taylor*	*1951*
Thirty-One Brothers and Sisters	*by Reba Paeff Mirsky*	*1952*
Tornado Jones	*by Trella Lamson Dick*	*1953*
Little Wu and the Watermelons	*by Beatrice Liu*	*1954*
Minutemen of the Sea	*by Tom Cluff*	*1955*
No Award		*1956*
Chucho, The Boy with the Good Name	*by Eula Mark Phillips*	*1957*
South Town	*by Lorenz Graham*	*1958*
Model A Mule	*by Robert Willis*	*1959*
"What Then, Raman?"	*by Shirley L. Arora*	*1960*
No Award		*1961*
Me and Caleb	*by Franklyn E. Meyer*	*1962*
No Award		*1963*
Across Five Aprils	*by Irene Hunt*	*1964*
No Award		*1965*
No Award		*1966*
Lions in the Way	*by Bella Rodman*	*1967*
Marc Chagall	*by Howard Greenfeld*	*1968*
Banner Over Me	*by Margery Greenleaf*	*1969*

 Manufactured in the United States of America. Published simultaneously in Canada by The Ryerson Press, Toronto.

Library of Congress Catalog Card Number: 58-13128

SEVENTH PRINTING

Standard Book Number: 695-48220-3 Library Binding

To my wife, Ruth,
who listened with me in the silences
and watched beside me in the dark places
and understood

SOUTH TOWN

1

David Williams and his little sister, Betty Jane, were hurrying along the highway toward South Town. They were walking northward on the left side. Traffic was always heavy along Route One, and they knew it was safer to face the traffic on their side. David strode along in front. Betty Jane trudged behind him, slipping and sliding when she stepped off the pavement. The highway was wet because it had rained earlier in the morning, and the red clay was soft and sticky.

It was early spring and warm, but they wore overcoats. Pneumonia weather, the people called it, chilly and damp for those who were idle, but mighty warm for those who had to walk three miles from home to school.

Usually they got a ride when they were on time, but they were late this morning Just as they were ready to leave, David had noticed that two of the pigs had got out of the pen. It had taken him and Betty Jane about fifteen minutes to catch them and shoo them back in again. David spent another five minutes fixing the break in the fence. Then both he and Betty Jane had to wash again and clean their shoes.

Mrs. Williams wrote a note to the teacher explaining why her children were late.

"We'll probably have to walk all the way," David said. "It's so late nobody will be passing now."

"I don't like being late for school," Betty Jane said.

"Then why don't you walk faster?" David asked.

"Walking fast enough to keep up with you."

"You are not. Dragging along behind, just holding me back."

"Started behind you."

"Come on then; let's stretch our legs. Be ten o'clock by the time we get there." David turned and swung into his stride, counting out the rhythm. "One-two-three-four! One-two-three-four!"

David kept counting, but at the same time he turned to look back at each car that overtook them. He was hoping some colored person would come along and pick them up. All the people who lived out that way knew the Williams family, and anybody would know David and Betty Jane were going to school, although David was as tall as a man. He was sixteen and growing. The trouser legs of the suit bought last fall hardly reached the tops of his heavy shoes.

They said David was like his father. He was slim, and his shoulders had not filled out yet, but he had his father's dark brown color and the same serious look in his eyes. Betty Jane was lighter. She was more like their mother, and her hair was smooth and black, like an Indian's.

Betty Jane hustled. She had to break step and run to keep up, for her short legs could not cover the distance her brother's could.

They were walking along a stretch of level road when David looked back at the sound of a roar which at first suggested the approach of a truck. It was not a truck but a glistening convertible traveling at high speed. It slowed as if the driver intended to stop — then it picked up speed and swung wide to the left as though out of control and bore down on the boy and girl where they had stopped off the pavement. Betty Jane jumped backward with a cry, tripping and falling sideways in the shallow ditch. The car passed with a nerve-shattering blast of the horn. In the rear window appeared two laughing faces as the convertible careened to the right again into its proper lane.

"Harold Boyd again!" David said.

He did not look at Betty Jane's face. She was not hurt, but as he went to pick up her book bag, he knew that she shared with him a bad feeling for which he had no words. It was something white folks made colored people feel when they could not fight back or talk or do anything but feel.

Harold Boyd was about the same age as David. He was

the son of the richest man in the county. His father's modern farm was within walking distance of the Williams' place, just a mile farther out from town. The families were well acquainted, for Mr. Boyd had the Ford agency and David's father had worked as a mechanic in Boyd's garage for years. During the past summer David had worked on the farm, and his mother had occasionally done house cleaning and nursing for the Boyds.

The families were well acquainted, but David did not like Harold. It was not because he was white or because his parents were rich. It was because of the thoughtless things he did. David knew the white boy had not actually meant to hurt him or Betty Jane, but he seemed to enjoy making people jump out of his way.

For another mile David and Betty Jane walked in silence. David carried the book bag, and he walked behind. He did not hurry, and he did not watch the cars that overtook them. So it was that the big car with the New York license plate overtook them and slowed before David noticed, but when it pulled off the pavement and stopped, he was watching.

"Rich white folks," he thought, "wanting to ask for information."

A colored chauffeur beckoned with his arm from his place at the wheel. David quickened his step, but he would not run. As he and Betty Jane drew nearer, he saw a pleasant-looking colored woman who called to them across the road.

"Are you children going to school?" It was the sweetest

voice David had ever heard. It was as though the woman was singing. She smiled and repeated her question; then she said, before David could answer, "You must be late. Come on. I'll give you a lift."

Now, David had been told not to get into the car of a stranger, but strangers meant people who were different. This lady in the fine car with a chauffeur — she was different, but when she smiled, she seemed just like folks you know. David took his sister's hand and ran across the highway. The chauffeur had left his seat. He was standing holding the door open very solemnly.

"Thank you, ma'am," David said. "We are going to school, and we're late. Sure was nice of you to pick us up."

The woman asked how far the school was. She asked what grade they were in.

"I'm in second year high, that's tenth grade. Betty Jane is in fifth grade. She's only nine, but she's right smart."

"And do you both go to the same school?"

"Yes'm," David said. "Pocahontas County Training School goes all the way from first grade through eleventh. It used to be only to tenth grade, but they raised it last year."

"Are you going to stay in school and graduate?" the woman asked.

"I'll have to graduate and then go away to school. You see, I'm going to be a doctor." David watched her face as he said it. Some people just laughed when he said he was going to be a doctor. There were no colored doctors in Pocahontas County. Everybody said it took too long, too many years in school, and it cost an awful lot of money to go away to college.

David was glad the woman did not laugh. She smiled, but in her eyes he could see she was not laughing at him.

"Why, that's wonderful," she said. Her voice was soft. He could never forget how she said it. "That's wonderful!"

She asked if they liked the school, and David said it was the best training school in that part of the state. She asked Betty Jane if she liked her teacher, and Betty Jane answered that she had the best teacher in the whole school and that last year she had thought she had the best teacher but this year she was sure her present teacher was the very best. The woman thought that was funny, and she laughed again. She laughed as though she were singing it, or as though a bird and not a person were laughing.

It was easy talking to her. Sure enough she was like home folks, but she was different, too.

Because the license plate announced that she was from New York, David explained that in Pocahontas County the schools for colored people were better than in some parts of the South. White children had better schools, but the public schools for colored children were considered very good.

Of course he did not know how good the schools were in other places, because he had not traveled, but people said that these schools were good.

"We have a new principal," he said. "He's from Indiana, and he went to school out there. He's trying to make the training school like the schools he went to."

"What do the people think about him?"

"Oh, they like Mr. Jackson. Everybody likes him." He paused a moment. "He's awful smart, smart and kind of hard too."

"David says he's harder on him than anybody else," Betty Jane piped up.

The woman smiled.

"Perhaps he thinks you require finer cutting," she said.

"Well, he knows my folks," David said. "My mother used to teach school, and she talks to him. He watches everybody, though." Then he added, as an afterthought, "He talks to you and makes you want to be something. He goes around to the people's homes. Most of the folks are poor, and they don't have much, but he goes in and visits with them."

"Every place he goes, they want him to eat something," Betty Jane added, "and they say he eats whatever's set before him and asks no questions."

They soon came to the hill where the school sat high on the left side of the road. Betty Jane pointed it out. A stranger might have gone by without seeing it. A great oak and a cluster of pine trees rose behind it, and the dark green of the building blended with the foliage. It was a pretty big school — just one story high, but it spread out. Still, David explained, it wasn't nearly big enough. Many of the rooms held two classes. There were three classes in the auditorium. There wasn't a real lawn, but the grass was not too high. A big American flag waved from the pole.

David and Betty Jane thanked the woman again and

said they could get out on the road, but the chauffeur turned in without the woman telling him what to do. David was glad the roadway was clean and the rocks bordering it were newly whitewashed.

"Oh, the jonquils!" the woman said. "And the paper flowers on the windows! Why, they are beautiful, and the windows are so clean that I can smell them."

David knew that it was like a figure of speech, but Betty Jane looked surprised.

They were getting out and saying their thank-you's all over again when Mr. Jackson came out. The principal's eyes got big when he saw what a fine car David and Betty Jane had come to school in. He took a step back and looked as if he wanted to go inside without saying anything, but the woman called out, "Good morning, Professor!"

"Good morning, Madam," Mr. Jackson said as he came forward.

"Please excuse the children for being late," she said. "I am afraid I kept them talking too long." She waved again as David and Betty Jane hurried in.

David went to his room. The teacher read his mother's note and handed it back to him, telling him to take it to the principal at recess time. As David walked toward his seat, Ben Crawford grinned at him and stuck his foot out in the aisle. David's toe hooked Ben's, and he went through the motions of falling and spun into his seat. It made the others laugh.

"This isn't a football field," Mrs. Booker said.

David glared at Ben. They were the best of friends.

The class was studying English, and Mattie Bowers was standing at her seat reading from *Ivanhoe.* There was a long description of Gurth, the swineherd. David had studied the lesson at home. It had been assigned for homework, but Mrs. Booker knew that few of her students opened their books outside of school.

David got his book open and found the place, but he kept thinking how much like singing the strange lady's voice was. He was remembering the way she talked and the queer things she said. Then he started thinking about the car. Gosh! His father would want to know about this colored woman traveling like that with her own chauffeur. Pa was an automobile man. He used to work at the Ford agency, and in the evenings he would tell the family about colored tourists who stopped there. He liked to serve them. He was proud of them when they were well-bred and when they spoke as though they were well educated.

David was imagining himself driving such a car going up Route One doing sixty, sixty-five, pushing his foot down a little more to seventy, seventy-five. She was smooth as kitten fur. Eighty miles an hour. If there wasn't a cop behind him on this straight road, well, give her the gun! Ninety, ninety-five, ninety-eight, ninety-nine, one hundred miles an hour. Split the wind, boy, she's wide open!

Mr. Jackson was at the door.

"David Williams, come, please."

The others looked at him. Shorty Johnston laughed.

Going to see the principal was bad business.

Mr. Jackson was standing at the door of the room called the office. He waited until David was in; then he followed and closed the door. The office was stuffy. The walls, except for one narrow window, were nothing but bookshelves. They said Mr. Jackson had read every book there, and lots more, too.

"Have a seat, David," the principal said. He was very serious.

David cleared his throat.

"Mr. Jackson, it wasn't just like the lady said," he began. "Really we were already late. Here is the excuse my mother wrote."

Mr. Jackson took the folded paper, but he laid it down without looking at it.

"She did not come from your home, then?"

No, sir, he had never seen her before. Yes, sir, she had stopped the car on the road, and he hadn't asked for a ride; he never hitchhiked. No, sir, she didn't say what her name was. Yes, sir, she sure was nice, and swell, not swell like being stuck up but swell like being awful good.

"Yes, I thought so too," Mr. Jackson said. He stretched his neck to look out of the window over David's head. "Good in a way . . . goodhearted. She said you spoke of the people looking up to the school and appreciating it."

"Well, I don't know." David was puzzled. "We talked about the school. I said the folks must like it, because they're sending their children. It's so crowded now. Before you came, folks didn't seem to care whether the kids came or not."

After he said it, David hoped Mr. Jackson wouldn't think he was trying to pass compliments.

"She was interested," the principal said. "She seemed to know something about this section. She understands conditions."

"Maybe she used to live around here. My mother would know her if she did." David would sure tell about her when he got home. "What's her name, Mr. Jackson?"

"I don't know. We talked a long time, but she didn't say. I started to ask, but she was talking, and I thought you would know her. Then she left, but before she drove off, she gave me something for the school." Mr. Jackson picked up something from the desk. It looked like a new dollar bill. He said, "David, have you ever seen one of these?"

"Why, yes, Mr. Jackson," he said. Everybody had seen new dollar bills.

"Look good, son." His hand was shaking, and David had to turn his head to one side. It still looked like a dollar bill until he read the words, "One Hundred Dollars."

"Gosh, Mr. Jackson," he said, getting up from his chair, "that's a hundred dollars all in one piece!"

"David, she left this for the use of the school. The lady wants us to paint the building white." He went on slowly. He was trying to remember just how she had said it. "She said a school like ours, sitting high on the hill by the side of the road, here in the dark country, should shine like a beacon. She said our school should ring out in the silences."

"The way she talks sounds funny, don't it, Mr. Jackson? It sounds queer, but when she says it, it's just right."

"Yes, David," Mr. Jackson said slowly as he rose. "It sounds queer but right, exactly right. Our school must ring out in the silences."

2

When Mrs. Williams called David on Saturday morning, she did not expect him to get right up. A full day's work lay ahead, so she called him at the same time as on school days. Then she made the fire in the shiny wood range and started breakfast. David heard the stove lids being moved. He wished his mother would wait a while. He felt a little ashamed of himself for not jumping up to make the fire. He decided he would just rest a little longer, and when he did start the day's tasks, he would be able to work harder.

Saturday! The springs squeaked as he turned toward the wall and went to sleep again.

"Come on, David." Ma was pulling the covers off him, and it was cold. "Come on, Son. It's almost seven o'clock."

2: SOUTH

"It's Saturday, Ma," David said, blinking in the sunlight as Ma ran up the shade. "We don't have to go to school."

"It may be Saturday for you, but Josephine and the pigs can't read calendars." Josephine was the one cow they kept for milk. Feeding Josephine and the pigs was regular before-school work. "Besides," Ma was saying as she went about her tasks in the kitchen, "you know Mr. Boyd said we could rent the tractor today. We musn't act like we don't want it. Come on and eat your breakfast before you feed up. Pancakes will be ready before your face is washed."

While David was dressing, he thought about the fright Harold Boyd had given Betty. They had said nothing to their mother about it. David hated Harold. He wanted to get even. He hoped that one day there would be a way. Sometimes he dreamed of elaborate and unrealistic changes, but he had no idea how such changes could be brought about.

"Gosh, we don't need to pay for a tractor to plow up that little garden. Looks funny putting a tractor on such a small piece. Why, there ain't hardly room enough to turn around in."

"What is 'ain't'? And you in high school!" Ma said from the kitchen. "Of course if you'd rather borrow a mule . . ."

"Never mind," David said quickly. "I'll get the tractor. It'll take me just about fifteen minutes, up one side and down the other. I'll let her out."

David's bedroom door opened directly into the kitchen. He sniffed the breakfast aroma as he went through the kitchen to the back porch to wash. It took only a little water in the tin basin for him to get clean. It was not half as much as Betty Jane would have used, but then his sister was just a little girl, and she didn't have to bring water in buckets from the well.

"All right, Josephine," he called in answer to a moo from the barn. "I'm a-coming, but I got to destroy a stack of pancakes for myself first."

The pigs in their pen beyond the barn heard David's voice, and they set up a noise as they fought to get the best places at their trough. While he stood brushing his teeth, David looked out, trying to figure how he would lay the rows when he got to work. The garden was toward the left of the house. The garage was to his right, on the side of the driveway from the road. Beyond the garage were the chicken house and the barn. Across the back of the four-acre tract, the land was left in pasture.

"Tomorrow Pa can tell us what he wants planted," David said as he went back into the kitchen. "You expect him home tonight, don't you, Ma?"

"I hope he'll get home," Ma said. She put a plate piled high with pancakes and strips of home-cured bacon on the oilcloth-covered table as David took his seat. "But we can't worry him with every little detail when he comes home. He ought to get some rest while he's here."

"Aw, he likes to work around home," David said.

"Well, he's working pretty hard down in the city all week, and lots of Sundays, too." Ma poured a glass of milk for her son and set the pitcher on the table so he could help himself to more. "I want him to rest when he's here. Besides, tomorrow's Sunday. It's not right working all day on the Lord's day."

"But he's making money," David said. "More than he ever made before, even when he was building ships."

"But it's not right. When he was working in South Town, we never did any work on Sundays, unnecessary work." Ma was thinking of the peace of other times when Ed Williams was really the head of the house. David was thinking of it too. It seemed a long time since his father had worked at the Ford place. He was known to be a good mechanic. During the war he had gone to the coast, where he worked at the shipyard. Later he had gotten a job in one of the new factories. It was not pleasant for the family, but the work was important, and the higher wages helped get the place paid for. There was not much land, not a farm, but it was large enough to grow vegetables and keep some stock. It kept David and his mother busy getting all the work done with Williams away.

After breakfast David fed up and milked. He liked to milk Josephine. The first *zing* of the stream of milk in the bottom of the shiny bucket always made a kind of funny feeling in his back between the shoulder blades. It *zinged* at first, and then when the bottom of the pail was covered, it sounded *zoup-zoup, zoup-zoup*. The last few, when the warm milk was foaming near the top of the bucket and the bag was nearly empty, went *pup-pup, pup-pup*. He liked those last short squirts. They were the periods.

TOWN

With his morning work finished, David started for the Boyd place, straight south on the highway. It was warm and he walked fast, so he wore no coat over his brown sweater and overalls. The visor of an old army cap sat smartly cocked over his right eye. By stepping along fast he could cover the distance in half an hour.

People called the Boyd place a model farm. Mr. Boyd called himself a gentleman farmer, but his business in the town interested him more than his farm. He held the Ford agency, and as the manager, he had really been Ed Williams' boss. Other business claimed his attention. It was said that he held more farm mortgages than the bank of which he was a director. During the tobacco season he bought and sold in the market.

Williams had said laughingly that Mr. Boyd might be a gentleman, but he was no farmer. It was a model farm which had boasted a private Delco electric system long before the government's rural electrification program had sent power lines through the country. The big white house was piped for running water. The bathroom and modern plumbing had been one of the wonders of the county. Plowing and working the land with a tractor, one man could cover more land than half a dozen men with mules.

Only in harvest time was Boyd really worried about help. Young men, both white and colored, had been drafted, and others had gone off to work in the shipyards and factories. Many families had moved to the North. Those left at home were hard put to it to keep their own land cultivated.

Whole families who had farmed on shares had moved away. Boyd and other landowners had argued until, as they themselves said, they were blue in the face. They had begged, threatened, and demanded, and the smiling poor said, "Yes, sir, you been good to us folks. No, sir, we ain't going to leave you all in the lurch."

That was what they said, but men went off to the cities saying that it was just to work a few weeks between times. Then they came and moved their families to the projects.

David's father had considered moving his family to the city. But he was not a tenant; he was buying his place. He called his four-acre plot "God's own acre," and he said he would rather have it for his home than a whole project in the city.

As David rounded the corner at the back of the Boyd house, he saw Harold playing ball with his cousin. Harold had on a new baseball uniform; even the spikes were new. He was heavier than David, but not so tall. The other boy was younger, about twelve years old. Everybody called him Little Red because of his unruly shock of red hair and his freckles. Little Red was wearing overalls and a faded blue shirt, but he was doing all right with the ball.

David thought of asking Harold about the tractor, but Harold hardly looked at him as he came into the yard, so he went up on the screened back porch and knocked at the kitchen door. There was the sound of someone moving about in the house, but the door was not opened. His hand was lifted to rap again when Mrs. Boyd opened the door.

"Well, I declare, boy," she said, "I thought sure you was Ruth Anne. What do you want?"

"No, ma'am, Mrs. Boyd," said David, taking off his cap. "I was looking for Mr. Boyd. He told Ma we could use the tractor today."

"Use the tractor?" She looked past David into the yard. "Who's going to drive it?"

"I am, Mrs. Boyd. Don't you remember how I drove it last summer when I worked for you all?" He hesitated. "I can handle it all right." There was no answer. He shifted his weight uncomfortably. "That is, if Mr. Boyd lets me take it."

"Oh!" Mrs. Boyd exclaimed as though she were offended. "Oh! You wanted to see him." She shut the door and turned away, leaving David wondering if he had said anything wrong.

He had only a few minutes to wait. Mrs. Boyd opened the door and silently held out the ignition key bound with copper wire to a stick. She did not hand the key to David. She held it dangling, and when he reached up for it, she let go quickly. Their hands did not touch.

Out at the barn, David knew what to do with the tractor. Driving the tractor was about the best part of the job. He checked gas and oil and kicked the tires. Everything was in order. He hooked on the plow unit and lifted it high so it would not drag when the back wheels lowered into the ditches. In the high driver's seat, his hand on the wheel, he felt like a part of the machine. With the motor going, his body thrilled to the vibration. The low muffled roar of the exhaust was like music.

He thought of going over to the small cottage to speak to old Hutch, the farm manager, but he did not want Mrs. Boyd to think he was fooling around. She was standing in the door watching. The machine moved smoothly along the drive that went by the house and toward the highway. Well, everything was in order. He looked back to see if the plow was hooked high enough. Nothing to it now.

Mrs. Boyd was saying something to him. He had to stop and shut off the motor to hear.

"I say tell your ma to come over and help me out. My Ruth Anne didn't come in today."

"Yes'm. I'll tell her," David said.

"She'll come right away, won't she?" Mrs. Boyd asked. "This is Saturday, and I have a lot of cleaning to do. Ruth Anne's let the house get dirty as a pigsty. She'll come right away, won't she, boy?"

"Well, I can't rightly say, Mrs. Boyd, but I'll tell my mother."

"I declare! Mighty independent she's getting since Ed went to working in the city. What's she got to do so much she can't work a day or two for me? What's she got to do today, I'd like to know?"

"Well, I don't know, ma'am," David said, "but she was busy when I left. I guess she's got some housework and some cooking to do — " he paused and added, "just like other folks."

"I don't know what's getting into you people. Biggity. Can't work any more . . . lazy."

"My mother isn't lazy, Mrs. Boyd," David said. "My mother never was lazy."

"Humph! She used to be glad enough to get a day's work." Mrs. Boyd had her elbows poked out with her hands on her hips. "You niggers are riding high now, but I'll see you eating humble pie one day. Your ma'll be looking for work one day."

"It's like I said, Mrs. Boyd." David did not want to argue, but he had to say it. "My mother has a lot of her own work to do, but I'll tell her you want her to come and help you out."

"And tell her I said right away," Mrs. Boyd called after him.

David drove home thinking. He did not enjoy the tractor at all for thinking about what Mrs. Boyd had said. His mother had a house to care for. She had baking to do on Saturdays. Pa would be driving in some time during the night, and Ma would want to have the house clean and good things ready to eat.

Betty Jane ran out to open the gate leading from the back yard into the section which was to be plowed. She was waving her arm and calling out as though to encourage him, "Come on, Dave! Come on, Dave!"

Today Betty Jane's clowning did not cheer him. As he had known, his mother was busy. She came to the back door with a broom in her hand. Her hair was protected from dust by a towel around her head. In a tub in the back yard David saw clothes that had been put to soak. Monday was washday, but every Saturday Ma said she had just a few little things to rub out. Lazy!

"What's the matter, David?" she asked as he walked up the steps. Ma could always tell if anything was wrong. "Did you have any trouble?"

"Well, kind of," David said slowly. "She wants you to work for her today."

"She who, David?"

"Mrs. Boyd says she wants you to help her out with her Saturday work because Miss Ruth Anne didn't show up this morning. She says for you to come right away." He added, "Gosh, she's mean!"

At first Mrs. Williams said she could not go, she had so much to do in her own house. David did not like to tell her all that was said, but Ma kept asking questions, "And what did you say?" and "Then what did she say?"

"I felt like telling her plenty," David concluded. "Talking about somebody being lazy because they don't want to scrub her dirty floors. We don't have to do it now. She's got her big house, and we got our little house, but it's our own and Pa's taking care of you so you don't have to go out for day work."

They had gone into the kitchen while they talked. Ma sat at the table. She reached up and started untying the cloth around her hair.

"Yes, it's our little house, and your father is working hard to take care of us, but" — Ma paused as she folded the cloth before her — "city work won't keep up forever, and we can't have folks thinking we're lazy. I guess I'll go over for a while."

"Ma, you can't do that," David said. "She just said that because she was vexed, vexed with her cook and maybe with us because we were renting a tractor instead of borrowing a mule."

"I'll do my work when I get back." His mother reached behind the door for her old coat. "I'll be ready by the time you get back up there with the tractor."

David started to protest again, but Ma kissed him full on the mouth and smiled. She told him to hurry up so he could come for her.

David went out and put the tractor in place. He lowered the plow unit and gave each plowshare a kick to start it into the ground. He climbed onto the seat and began his first row at the edge of the plot. As he turned at the end of the row, he saw his mother walking up the highway. She walked erect with her head tilted back.

"Lazy!" David said, as though speaking to the tractor. "She ain't got a lazy bone in her body."

At the top of the hill Ma turned and waved, and David stood up and lifted his cap and waved it in a circle over his head.

3

Saturday nights were usually cheerful at the Williams house. If Mrs. Williams had not been called upon to clean an extra house that day, she would have been lively and happy. They said little about it, but David could see that his mother was tired. During the day Betty Jane had gone on with the house cleaning. She had swept and dusted and put clean sheets on the beds. When David took the tractor back, Ma was not ready to leave. It was a big house, and Mrs. Boyd wanted many things done. Ma had come out to the back yard with a piece of cake and a glass of milk. She had said very little, and David had not seen any of the Boyds.

David was pressing his suit. He was hoping it would be warm on Sunday, so he would not have to wear his overcoat.

It was shabby, and the sleeves were way up on his arms.

Mrs. Williams was shaping loaves of bread in their pans. A cake was already baking in the oven, and the warm kitchen smelled of vanilla. They liked their kitchen. It was bright with electricity from the government's power line that stretched from pole to pole along the highway. The light from the globe overhead made the nickel trimming of the stove shine like silver. It was reflected again from the rows of cans on the shelf and from the row of aluminum pans on the wall beside the dull iron skillets.

Betty Jane was begging to be allowed to stay up until her father came home, but Mrs. Williams said, "We don't even know that your father is coming."

"But he didn't come last week," said Betty Jane, "so he's got to come tonight."

"Lots of week ends he didn't get home last winter," David said. "Worked right on through Sundays, same as any other day."

"But they don't work so many Sundays now," his mother said. "Maybe the work will run out soon."

"I wish it would be over right away," said Betty Jane. "Then Pa could be with us all the time. Ma, don't you miss Pa something awful?"

"Yes, I miss him all right," Ma said, smiling at her daughter. "I miss him, and so do we all, but we're the lucky ones. Think of the families where the man of the house is in the army or the navy, and when there's war many of them are killed. We're blessed. We have a lot to be thankful for."

David put his coat on the back of a chair and started in on the trousers. Trousers were easy to press. He always liked to do the hardest part of his work first. As he carefully brushed them and then laid the cloth over them and dampened it, he thought about something good to come out of military service.

"They get good training in the army." He hoped his mother would not think he was just arguing. He liked to talk with her. "They teach all kinds of trades. They teach auto mechanics and aviation. Why, they say it costs twenty thousand dollars to make an army pilot."

"Yes, David," Ma agreed. "Twenty thousand dollars to make a flyer. That's more than Pocahontas County Training School cost to build. It's more than it costs to run the school for a whole year. If people didn't have so much hate in their hearts, the training school could be really equipped, and we could have enough teachers so you and Betty Jane could get the kind of education you need. You could really be preparing for medical school."

Ma opened the oven door and took the sweet-smelling cake out. She slid the pans of bread in and put more wood on the fire. She turned the cake out of the pan and fitted its soft bulk on a wide plate. As she started to make the icing, she went on with her thoughts.

"Just suppose, David," she said, "suppose instead of spending all the money for war it was turned to training for peace. Suppose farm boys went away to agricultural schools or to trade schools. Suppose the army doctors and nurses and hospitals were spread out for the health of the people. Suppose all the jobs could be for some use other than destroying."

"That," said Betty Jane, who had been listening intently to everything, "that would be like heaven."

By eleven o'clock Betty Jane was nodding, and her mother sent her to bed. David finished his Saturday night work. His suit was pressed, and the shoes were shined. He took a tub from the back porch into his room and had his bath. Ma told him to go on to bed. She said she was not going to wait up for his father. She admitted she was tired.

"David," Ma called from the kitchen after he was in bed, "I didn't tell you about Mrs. Boyd." Her voice was strained. She had hardly spoken of what had been said during the day at the Boyd place. "I guess she's upset. Ruth Anne sent word she wouldn't be there tomorrow, so Mrs. Boyd asked me to come back."

David lay still. A lump came up in his throat. It wasn't right. Ma shouldn't have gone for one day, even. She didn't have to. Ma went on.

"She got right mad when I said I couldn't." When he heard that, David felt better. "I tried to make her understand, but I guess it was no use."

4

When David woke up the next morning, he knew it was late. He knew right away that his father had come in during the night and that he had gotten up and started the morning work. Sunday! Pa sure liked to work around the house on his Sundays at home. Maybe Mrs. Boyd would say he was lazy, too. David laughed at the thought.

David could hear his father's deep voice from the kitchen, although the door was closed. It had been left open the night before. Somebody must have closed it to keep out the noise so he could sleep. Well, he had slept all right, but you just couldn't stay in bed all day, even if it was Sunday. Besides, he was hungry.

His mother was taking a pan of muffins from the oven

when he went through the kitchen to the back porch to wash. She said his father was feeding the chickens. That would mean the cow and the pigs had already been fed. As David went out, he saw Pa coming up the path. David loved his father, and he was proud of him. He had never talked about being proud of him, or about loving him either. It was just natural.

Ed Williams was not so tall, but he was straight and muscular. He walked as though he knew where he was going, and he worked steadily as though he did not find it necessary to stop and think or question in his mind the next thing to do. He was like one of the efficient motors he liked to work on.

"A man ought to be better at what he does than a machine," he sometimes said. "A man's got everything a machine has, and then he's got a brain to control it."

"How's tricks, boy!" he said as he came up the back steps to slap David on the back and shake his hand.

They talked about spring planting, the richness of Josephine's milk, the amount of food the pigs were eating, and how they were growing. David talked as he splashed water over himself. He did not fail to notice that Pa had even filled the water buckets.

Betty Jane ran out in her nightgown to throw her arms around her father's neck. It was different with girls. They loved their fathers and said so and said how and when they were proud of them.

Mrs. Williams called her family to breakfast, and both Betty Jane and David hurried to get dressed.

Pa said he had brought his appetite with him. There was nothing anyplace to equal Ma's cooking, pass the muffins, Son. He sure could eat. He laughed and made them laugh. Sunday breakfast with Pa in the house was fun. David thought of how it would be now if his mother had gone to work for Mrs. Boyd that morning. He wished he could tell about it, but he knew it would spoil things. Besides, it looked like Ma had completely forgotten.

Pa said, "The way Dave's eating, I know he won't want any dinner."

But Ma said, "Dinner? The boy will be hungry as soon as he leaves the table." David had to smile, because it was really true. He was always hungry.

The family sat about the breakfast table there in the kitchen and talked of many things. Outside it started raining, slow and drizzly at first and then heavier, as though it meant to keep falling all day. Pa talked some about the city and his work there, but he asked a lot of questions, too. He wanted to hear the others talk. He said he had to pick up enough to last him a while.

Betty Jane started telling about the strange lady who rode in a fine Cadillac and said funny things. Pa asked for all the details, and David described the wonders of the car with push buttons to raise and lower the windows and to open the doors.

Then Pa started talking about the city again.

"Over to the new colored high school they have courses at night. I've been going to the classes in automobile mechanics," Pa said. "There are some mighty fine people around there, and all kinds of shops for training. David, you ought to see the place. You'd like it."

"Couldn't I go with you, Pa?" David asked. "I could get a job for the summer and live with you at the dormitory."

"David's no man. David's just a boy," Betty Jane said.

"He's getting on, though." Pa defended his son's ambitions. "He's getting on, and I want him to get outside and see. Everything's different down there. The schools are different, the people are different, the way they go about, even the way they think."

"Gosh," said David, "I sure wish we could go there to live."

"You know, I've been thinking," Pa went on, "I've been doing a lot of thinking. Being in a place like that gives you a chance to sort of see. Of course it's still in the South, but between looking at things and talking with people, you see what we're missing in South Town." He paused, but no one else spoke. They wanted him to go on.

"It seems like here we are on Route One, main highway from north to south. People pass through, big cars, little cars, jalopies and trucks. Sometimes they stop to buy gas and oil and maybe stay overnight. We look at them, and we speak to them, but we don't get to know them. We don't get the chance to exchange ideas with them. We don't get the chance to improve ourselves, to be what they have gotten to be.

"Now you tell me about this lady," he went on. "She must be somebody, I mean she must really be somebody.

Maybe her husband is a business man or a college president or a doctor. She comes by, and she says some things that sound funny to us because they are different. She sees the schoolhouse, and she knows it's important. She wants it to look important, and she planks down the money for paint. I'd like to know more about her. I'd like the kids to know more. I'd like them to have better schooling than they're getting."

"Dear, you know I said if you thought best we could move to the city," Ma said. "I'd be glad to go." She looked over at David, and he knew his mother would be glad to get away from Mrs. Boyd and people like her.

"Sure, Pa," said David, and Betty Jane was voicing her approval too. "I'd like that. Going to a real city school."

"That ain't the answer." Pa shook his head. "Things change faster in the city than in the country, but it's got disadvantages too. Crowding, slums, and more Jim Crow than out here. At least we're not bothered with white folks. No, we're getting the place paid for, and I'm looking for the answer. I'm truly seeking for a way out. But, Ma, we got to fix it so the kids can see." He shoved back his chair and looked at his son. "Dave, let's go out and look around," he said. "Get your coat. I want to show you how you can fix that broken place in the fence so the pigs can't get out."

David and Betty Jane did not go to Sunday school. Mrs. Williams was a Sunday school teacher, but when her husband was at home, she wanted to spend all her time with him. Besides, it was raining and few children would be present.

They did go to church later. It was preaching Sunday. The Oak Grove church was on a dirt road a mile from the highway. The minister lived in the next county and came regularly on the third Sunday of each month to preach to his people. He came at other times when there was sickness or death or special need, and for one week each year he came to hold revival services. Reverend Arrington was short and stout and very dark in color. His bald head seemed too large for his body. In spite of his great weight, he moved with energy, and when he preached it was with his heavy arms waving and his feet stomping as he went from one side of the pulpit to the other.

The people said he was a good man, and they loved him.

Preaching Sunday was a big day in the month's routine of the community. Mr. and Mrs. Williams sat with Betty Jane down near the front. David sat on the last seat near the door, with his friends. He saw others in church who, like his own father, were holding jobs away from home. They liked to get back for the third Sunday because they would meet again, and in the afternoon they would visit from house to house.

His father had talked that morning about seeing, and now Reverend Arrington's sermon had a lot in it about the same thing. He preached about those who have ears to hear and hear not and eyes to see and see not.

David always liked the first of Reverend Arrington's sermons. He would start by explaining. He compared the condition of those who were deaf or blind with the privileges of normal people who could go about their duties with full enjoyment of their blessings. He told the story of a blind piano player who had said that only when he heard the melodies of his instrument could he see the blueness of the sky and the glisten of sunshine dancing on the waters. David thought of how the lady in the Cadillac had spoken of smelling the beauty of paper flowers pasted on clean windows. He could understand what the blind man might mean.

Then the preacher went on to talk about the many people who had their sight and yet never really saw the blue of the sky, of people who could not enjoy the beauty of a green field or thrill to stand between rows of high waving corn and know that God had raised up something more than a crop.

David had never thought about corn that way, but he remembered that when he was younger and they lived at his grandfather's, he had loved to play in the tobacco rows. The plants grew up higher than his head, and the ground was kept free of grass and weeds. In hot midsummer he had stomped barefooted along the rows and imagined himself a giant stalking through a forest of great oak trees. He knew it was good, but he had not thought of it as beauty. The reverend recited the poem,

I think that I shall never see
A poem lovely as a tree.

David knew the words. They often sang it in school, and as the preacher intoned the words, the tune was going through David's mind. He hummed very softly. He thought he was humming softly, but Ben Crawford nudged him, and he realized that he had been too loud.

The recitation ended that part of the sermon. There was a noticeable stirring all over the church. One of the boys with David said, "Now here comes the gravy!"

The other boys laughed, and they whispered and shifted in their seats.

Toward the front of the church, too, they knew what was coming to revive their dull spirits. Many of the older people enjoyed only loud preaching. They wanted to feel themselves stirred by great sound and forceful exhortation. They sat up in anticipation. An occasional "Amen" had been heard, and with the reading of the poem the rhythm had moved Sister Elizabeth Padmore to pat her foot. Now she cried out, "Preach, boy, preach!"

Reverend Arrington laid aside his notes and prepared to preach.

His voice was full and rich. He was heavy, but he moved lightly on his feet, and when he started really preaching he gasped audibly at the end of each phrase as air rushed in to refill his lungs. His voice rose and fell in a cadence. His message was filled with phrases which were beautiful not for what they said but for the rich meaning they had for his hearers.

Some folks are so mean, ah,
That all about them, ah,
They can't see a thing that's good, ah.
They walk around searching for trouble,

And picking faults in all that they see.
Holy God Himself,
I say God in Heaven can't please such folks.
If He sends down the blessed twinkling rain
To wash the old world's dirty toil-worn face
And dampen down our thirsty crops a-standing
in the fields,
Some folks calls it nasty weather.
And look-a here, look-a here:
When the celestial sun turns his smiling
countenance on the earth
In all his magnificent glory
And bounces his beams off'n the rolling hilltops
And charges the sleeping valley with abounding energy
Some folks say, "Ain't it hot!"
Yes! Yes!

Reverend Arrington preached. He stomped across his platform. He shook his fist and pounded on the pulpit. He talked about the evil of mankind, the selfishness and hate.

Strong man takes from the weak man,
Him that hath taketh from him that hath not
Even that little that he seemeth to hath,
White man takes from the black man
And black man takes from his brother.

That's why, he said, war rages throughout the world. He described the agonies of battle, the terror of bombs falling on the innocents, the bombs that flew on the wings of hate guided by the cunning of Satan himself and carrying Hell's own fire and brimstone. He put in his own sound effects, and they were good.

The people were called upon to open their eyes and to open their ears, to see the glory and hear the word. Reverend Arrington quoted long passages of scripture, the promises, the hope, the faith. At one place he threw back his head and sang. All the people joined in, and it looked like the church itself rocked as he swayed from side to side.

Oh yes, Oh yes.
Our young folks are walking in darkness.
They're seeking, but they don't know what
they're looking for.
They say they're looking for a good time
And they're rushing hell-bent for destruc-
tion.
Our girls are going off to the big city
And in the night I see them, going in
and out
Where the lights are burning bright
And the jazz music is blasting out so loud
they can't hear,
They can't hear the still small voice say-
ing to them
"Be still. Be still, I say, and know that
I am God."

Sister Padmore had been crying out her loud amens. Others were leaning forward and drinking in the words. They were feeling as well as hearing the sermon. There was no question about anyone sleeping now. When, at the end of loudness designed to shout down the blasting of jazz music, Reverend Arrington dropped his voice to a whisper to give a vivid impression of the still small voice, Sister Padmore screamed in her excitement. She jumped to her feet and turned about as though she would fall. No one tried to restrain her, and she continued to stand. Deacon Robertson, whose grown children had all gone to the northern cities, wept noisily in fear of the temptations they were facing.

Reverend Arrington went on to talk about gossiping tongues and scandalizing talebearers. He lashed out at backbiters and rogues, at drunkards and wife-beaters. Then at the height of his attack, when half the members of his congregation were lost with him in the frenzy of their emotion, he stopped and said simply, "Let us pray."

He grasped the pulpit with both hands and bowed his head. The shouters quieted somewhat. Sister Padmore sat down exhausted. Another who had been shouting was leaning back in her seat as though in a faint. A man was fanning her with his hat. David bowed his head, but he did not close his eyes. He knew there was a great power in words. Reverend Arrington could sure make the old folks shout, but he made the people understand, too. He made them understand some things. David had learned something about seeing. He determined he would be seeing more things, listening for more things. Some day he would be able to teach the people, to make his own voice ring out in the silences.

The short prayer was softly spoken, so softly that David did not hear all the words.

". . . Give us that love that runs from heart to heart like a sweet potato vine runs from hill to hill . . . and finally, Lord, when we can't do no more here below, finally, when the bed sheet becomes a shroud, when the stammering tongue is clove to the roof of the mouth and our toil-worn hands are crossed in rest, take us up, finally, O Lord, to that mansion not made with hands but eternal in the heavens. This is our prayer. Amen."

David leaned over and said to Ben, "The man sure can preach," and Ben agreed.

"I got to go out," Ben said. "Come on, let's catch some air."

David started to leave with Ben and many others who were moving toward the door, but the organist played the introduction of a hymn, and the choir started singing. It was one of David's favorite songs. It had harmony, and he liked to sing the tenor. "You go ahead. I'll be out later."

There were no songbooks in the pews, but everybody knew the words. David wondered why the choir members always looked at their books and seemed lost without them. He was sure most of them could not read music, and he knew some of them could not read anything.

The preaching did not end the service. There were many announcements, more singing, collections, and a long talk by Brother Dan Jenkins, who was the government farm agent.

All the people liked Brother Dan. He was a farmer like

the others, but he was an educated man, a graduate of Tuskegee Institute. He helped the people with advice and instructions, working sometimes for days at a stretch to help establish a new farm plan, making the first cut with the plow to establish contour lines, swinging an axe to show a better way of felling trees. He was thin to the point of looking sickly, but no one had heard of his spending a day in bed, and stronger looking men could not keep his pace.

He boasted that he knew every grown person in the county, white and colored. Each Sunday he attended one of the churches where they were having preaching. He would give out information and advice according to the season, warning the farmers sometimes about setting tobacco plants too close and advising them against repeating crops on the same land. He would give the right prices for fertilizers and supplies and explain government farm regulations. While he spoke, many in the church would move about and turn to talk with neighbors. It was not because they did not respect Brother Dan. There was just so much to be said among people who assembled only on third Sundays.

While Brother Dan talked, David went out to join those who stood about the churchyard under trees dripping with softly falling rain.

Ben's father, Israel Crawford, home for the day from his job in the city, was saying that preaching was all right, but somebody with book learning and a speaking voice as good as Reverend Arrington's should be holding organizing meetings to wake the folks up.

"We got to get together," he said. "We ought to have some kind of organization so a man could have protection. If we work their land, they cheat us out of our share. If we work our own land, they buy our sorry crops at their own price."

Crawford argued that the folks could get together and demand contracts. They could buy and sell together and get more land for themselves. Then, he said, if one man got in trouble, it would be easy for all to help him, to fight for him.

"Somebody got to do it," he concluded, "but it'd take a man, a real man, one with guts and learning too."

The Williamses ate an early dinner on Sundays. Ma sometimes said that they just ate all day, because when they got back from church, everybody was hungry, especially David. He had to have sandwiches and milk. Later when dinner was served in the dining room with the good dishes, David was ready again. He ate his share of stewed chicken and dumplings, candied sweet potatoes, and steaming spoon bread, followed by peach cobbler with whipped cream.

After dinner Pa lay down to take a nap. He would be leaving at midnight for the drive back to the city. Ma and Betty Jane started washing the dishes. When they got through, they would look at the Sunday paper and the weekly *Afro-American* Pa had brought home. David went up to the crossroads, where he was to meet some of the boys. It had stopped raining. He and Ben could go for a walk or maybe pick up a ride and go wherever the driver might be going.

They did not ride, but they did go down the road as

far as the Mannings', stopping and talking with others on the way. Mrs. Manning had heard about the school's visitor and her gift. She wanted all the details from David and asked him a lot of questions he could not answer. How tall was the lady? What did she wear? Where had she been, and where was she going? David told all he knew, but he said he guessed he was one of those the preacher had talked about, one who has eyes and sees not.

David was on his way back home after his Sunday visiting when he saw Mr. Boyd's car pull up in front of the house. He heard the horn blow. A moment later his father walked down the front steps and out to the car, stopping to shut the gate behind him. When David got closer and started to pass, his father called him.

"David," he said, "Mr. Boyd is telling me that you gave his wife some back talk yesterday."

"Who? Me?" David asked, surprised. After he said it, he knew it sounded silly but . . .

"Of course you," Mr. Boyd said, shifting his cigar. "Mrs. Boyd was right upset by your saucy manners. She didn't want me to say anything, but Ed's a good boy, and I don't want to see his young one and his woman getting into trouble."

"My wife? What's she got to do with it?" Pa asked.

"He started trouble," Boyd said, pointing at David. "Gave my wife some fast talk about his ma. Then when your woman came up there to work, she backed him up — and she wouldn't come back to help out today — refused good money for her services — too uppity I call it."

Pa was puzzled. He looked from Boyd to David and back again.

"My wife? Working for Mrs. Boyd?"

"Sure! And arguing with her! Didn't she tell you?" Boyd thrust his head out.

"Maybe she did say something." Pa spoke slowly. "Yes, I guess she did. I just didn't pay it no mind."

Boyd got out his billfold.

"Here, Ed, here's her pay. Four dollars, my wife said, and no hard feelings. It's just the boy."

Williams drew back and put his hands in his pockets. "No," — he shook his head — "no, I can't take it. It's between the women."

"You refuse my money?"

"If my wife didn't take it, she had her reasons. No — I can't take it."

"So! It's you and the boy!" Boyd's face was red. "High-faluting! Big time! I don't know what's getting into you folks, but we'll find a way to take it out of you. You!!" He turned toward David. "What you need is a good horsewhipping. You got to learn to respect white people, boy. I won't have you talking back to my wife, and no other white man will. You better talk to that boy, Ed. You better tell him to stay in his place, or by the Lord other men will show him."

Boyd stepped on the gas. The wheels spun and showered gravel on David and his father as Boyd drove off.

"Son, you got me on the spot," Pa said. "Why didn't you let me know about this mess?"

"It wasn't anything to tell," David answered. "We figured we wouldn't bother you. Here comes Ma now, but Pa, she was right."

They went into the house and talked. David told everything that he and Mrs. Boyd had said that Saturday morning, trying hard to remember the exact words. Ma backed him up, but she did not tell everything she had said or what the other woman had said to her.

Pa said that they had done right, right in everything except not telling him about it.

"After all," he concluded, "it makes me feel kind of small hearing about it first from that white man and not knowing how to answer him. But never mind. Lots of white folks are rebbish like that, still fighting the Civil War and wanting colored folks to act like slaves. They're mean and dangerous. We got to keep away from that kind much as we can."

"I should have really said something to her," David said.

"No," his mother cut in, "I'm the one to talk to her."

"Well, she asked for it," David went on. "Next time I'll tell her."

"No, Davie boy." Pa laid his hand on David's arm and felt the quivering of his muscles. "No, don't let there be another time. For God's sake, don't. I've always tried to protect you and I always will, and whatever you do, I'm with you, but . . . just keep away from people like her. That's about all you can do, keep away from them."

5

The news of the school's visitor and the gift had spread throughout the county. By the time the children had carried the story home and it had been discussed from house to house, from church to church, and from store to store, those who had it firsthand would not have recognized the tales.

The school league met on the night of the first Monday in each month. When next it rolled around, attendance was more than satisfactory. The two school buses made their routes, and this time they could not bring all who wanted to come. Parents came in cars and in wagons drawn by horses and mules, and many who lived nearby came on foot. It was a clear night, but there was no moon. David, with his mother, was among those who arrived early. He looked down the hill to watch the slow-moving lights from lanterns carried by those who walked.

David knew that in many school leagues the teachers took the leading part. Usually a parent, or patron as they were called, would be elected president, but the real responsibility would fall to the principal. In the Pocahontas County Training School League the farm agent, Brother Dan Jenkins, was president. He had been president ever since David had known anything about it. Mrs. Williams was secretary. David thought it was wonderful the way his mother always got everything down on the record. When she read the minutes of the last meeting, nobody ever said she had made a mistake. Ma was on the ball.

She would read from her book, holding it high like a student on exhibition day. "The meeting opened at eight o'clock with the president in the chair. Mr. Samuels led in prayer. This was followed by the singing of "Amazing Grace How Sweet The Sound," led by Sister Cora Smith . . ."

Her clear voice would go on, and everyone would stop talking to listen. Not many children attended, but those who had come with their parents would look at David, and he would have to hold himself to keep from showing that he was proud of his mother.

Tonight the meeting really did open at eight o'clock. The president was in the chair, and all the seats in the auditorium were filled. While Mrs. Williams read the minutes, the rattle of dishes and the smell of frying fish were the only distractions. In the home economics room Miss Burton was busy with some of the older girls preparing to sell refreshments. People would want fish sandwiches and cold drinks in the half hour of socializing after the meeting.

Opening formalities were soon over. There was a report by a committee that had visited the school board asking for an addition to the building. David thought that the board must get very tired of seeing such committees. At almost every league meeting, plans were being made to present such requests, or reports of further delay were being brought in.

The finance committee reported its purchase of additional supplies for the home economics department. The secretary read the list, naming each item and giving the prices. Scissors, new bobbin for the sewing machine, so many spools of thread, cloth for making dish towels, a meat grinder.

Brother Dan called on the principal for a special report. All the audience gave their full attention while Mr. Jackson told about the unusual visitor, her interest in the welfare of the people, her desire to have the school building more attractive, her gift of a hundred dollars for paint. He suggested that a committee be appointed to purchase paint and that a day be set when all the men who could wield a brush should assemble at the school to do the job.

A day in the Easter vacation was agreed on. It would be warm, and they hoped it would not rain. Someone consulted a calendar to see in what phase the moon would be. The farmers did not want to come at a time when they had to be planting. Brother Dan had often said that the phase of the moon had nothing to do with success or failure of planting, but they did not believe him.

On the appointed day the buses made their circuits, and again they could not bring all who wanted to work. Men came to paint, and women came to bring food and to visit with relatives and friends. From early morning, brushes were going. Brother Dan was in charge. The farm-and-shop teacher was really doing the work of seeing that the paint was mixed right and that each man understood his job, but it was Brother Dan who did most of the talking. He pretended to be a hard taskmaster. He rushed around scolding and calling the men lazy, especially those who were most industrious.

"I sure like to see Brother Dan running about," a woman said. "Why, the man is worth his weight in gold."

"Well, he ain't worth much then," Sister Padmore said, " 'cause a good stiff breeze would blow him away. I mean way away. He ain't more than enough to hang britches onto."

They laughed at him, but they liked him all right.

When the whistle at the sawmill blew for twelve o'clock, everybody stopped to eat. It was like a picnic. Someone had brought a pig to barbecue over an open fire. Some of the women had gone into the schoolhouse to fry chicken. Others had brought baked ham and sweet potato pie and a dozen kinds of cake.

Mr. Jackson moved from group to group, eating whatever he was offered. He had been painting along with the others, but Brother Dan said he had gotten more paint on his clothes than he had on the building.

At one o'clock they went back to work. They wanted to finish the job in one day. In the morning there had been talk and laughter and singing. Now men eyed the unpainted sections, and when they spoke, it was only about getting through.

David left his place on a ladder at the back to refill his paint bucket. At the front of the building women were putting the last of their pans and dishes into baskets. Down on the highway a car slowed to stop, then backed to the driveway and turned in. David watched the approach. The driver was a white man. He was leaning from the window and stretching his neck to look as the car came up the hill.

"What's going on here?" the man shouted, even before he braked to a stop and got out. David recognized him as Mr. Barker, chairman of the school board.

"We just painting our school," a man near him replied with a broad smile. "Look nice, don't it?"

"Who told you to?" the chairman demanded, but he did not wait for an answer. The principal was coming around the corner wiping his hands on a rag. "Jackson, what's going on here?" he demanded.

"Good afternoon, Mr. Barker," the principal said. "The people were trying to give the community a surprise. We've needed paint for a long time."

"Surprise? Surprise? It is a surprise!" His face was red, and he was waving his arms. "Why wasn't I consulted about this? Where's the money coming from? Who authorized you to tamper with the county's property?"

"Why, Mr. Barker —" Mr. Jackson was speaking low,

but no one stirred and they could all hear his words — "it isn't costing the county one cent. A friend donated money for the paint, and people are giving their labor. The good people of the county should be pleased."

"You don't have to tell me how the good people of the county should feel. I'm the county chairman, and I should have been consulted. Now who is this philanthropist that goes around giving away paint?"

"I really don't know," Mr. Jackson said. He was still speaking low, though Mr. Barker was talking loud with anger in his voice. "I really do not know the name. She left the money in cash."

Mr. Jackson told once again how the woman had brought two of the children to school on a rainy day and with no suggestion from him said she would like to pay for the painting of the building. She had offered to pay the whole cost, but he had accepted only enough to cover cost of materials.

"Jackson —" at last Mr. Barker had lowered his voice — "Jackson, I ought to have you fired," he said.

Brother Dan had come up to stand beside the principal. He had been nodding agreement as the story was told.

"Mr. Barker, you got no cause to vex yourself," Brother Dan said with a smile. "Professor here hasn't done anything bad. Of course we should have consulted you. I'm president of the school league. It was my duty to tell you. I'll take that blame."

"Why, you don't even know who the woman was," Mr.

Barker said. "She might have been a spy, going around picking up colored children in her car. A Communist. That's what she is. I know she's a foreign Communist trying to spread race dissension among the Negroes." He pronounced the word as though it were spelled "niggers." Somebody laughed on the edge of the crowd.

"No, sir, Mr. Barker. She wasn't one of them foreigners," Brother Dan said. He tried to laugh. "Why didn't you tell him, Professor?"

"It happens that the lady was a colored American." Mr. Jackson was the one who was angry now. "Does that make a difference?"

"Well, all fire! Why didn't you say so, man?" Mr. Barker was calming down, but he wasn't silent long. "Who was she to come interfering with our business in Pocahontas County?"

"She seemed only to be a friend who was interested in the progress of our people." The principal added, "White or colored, it would have been the same to me."

The county chairman snapped back his head and took a step forward.

"Jackson, I'm telling you," he said, "you may be smart in books, but you got a lot to learn. It does make a difference whether folks are white or black. It makes plenty difference in Pocahontas County. Get that through your head."

He turned toward the farm agent.

"Dan, I blame you for not coming to me about the whole business," he said. As Mr. Barker walked back to the car, someone laughed. With his hand on the door, he turned.

"Jackson," he said, "I want a full written report for the board. And you find out who that nigger woman was."

As the car rolled down the hill, the principal stood with his head back, his eyes fixed on a passing cloud, or perhaps he looked beyond. Brother Dan Jenkins, who had lived in the county all his life, was saying to him that, after all, Mr. Barker should have been consulted.

Everybody had stopped work. The men were slow in getting started again. They did not talk much. They did not discuss Mr. Barker. They worked, but their task seemed less pleasant. Brother Dan ran back and forth with his urging. Where he stopped, they laughed again, and picked up speed.

"Come on there, old man Williams," he cried, shaking the ladder on which David was standing to do his share. "Come on, old man Williams. You ain't moved in so long I thought you was just a black spot waiting for paint. We got to get this job finished. What you reckon I'm paying you ten dollars a day to do?"

Later in the afternoon Brother Dan went to old man Ezra Simmons, who really was too old to get on a ladder. It was said he was the father of twenty children, and grandfather and great-grandfather to more than he could count. He had come wanting to help, so he had been given a brush and a bucket, but he stood on the ground painting the lower part of the side wall.

Brother Dan went to old Simmons and he said, "Lord have mercy! They done robbed the cradle and sent a boy to do a man's work. Look out there, little Ezra, you better mind how you get in the road of these big men. They be stepping on you directly."

The old man laughed so hard he had to set his bucket down and lean against the building. He had no teeth, and when he laughed his mouth was a yawning well of darkness. He laughed, and the whole thing was funny to others and they stopped to laugh with him. That made the old man laugh still harder, and tears rolled down his sunken cheeks. He put up his hand to wipe his eyes. He forgot that the brush, wet with paint, was in his hand. He smeared his face with white paint, and then he was a sight that made everybody, men and women, young and old, laugh until they could not control themselves. Those who came from the other side of the building ran back to call their friends to come and see. Old man Simmons tried to clean his face and only made himself look more ridiculous. Jacob Slaughter fell off a ladder. Women held their sides and laughed. The fat ones sank to the ground and rocked and rolled. Brother Dan lost his power to make men work. For the rest of the day little was accomplished, and those who lived nearby had to return the next day to finish.

And when the job was finished, all the people of the county said the training school shone like the rising sun.

It was some weeks later that David saw the picture. He was looking at a weekly magazine, and there in full color was a picture of a famous soprano. In the picture she was smiling just as David remembered her that day in the car. Now he knew why her voice was like the singing of birds.

6

David was eating his breakfast when Betty Jane called from the front door.

"Come on, Dave! Here comes Mr. Crayton."

"Hurry, Son!" his mother said. "You mustn't keep him waiting."

"Good gosh!" David said between mouthfuls. "Most days he's late — sometimes he don't come at all — now he's ahead of time. He makes me tired."

Just the same, he hurried.

When he climbed into the car beside the farm-and-shop teacher, only the Manning girl was in the back seat with Betty Jane.

"Where's the rest of your riders?" he asked.

"Well, you know how it is," Mr. Crayton said. "It's planting time and good weather."

David did know how it was. As they drove toward the school, the newly plowed land lay brown and raw on both sides of the highway. A farmer behind his mule was laying rows, curving to follow the rise of the hill. Contour plowing, they had learned to call it. Along the rows boys and girls, each with a basket of tender young tobacco seedlings, were setting out the plants. From the fields they waved and called out as the car went by. Those who stayed out of school seemed to be enjoying themselves.

"There's not much you can do about it," Mr. Crayton said. "In some counties they close school for two weeks in the spring. That doesn't help, though. The farmers still keep the kids out. They figure it's a waste of time to have their young ones in school when they could be making cash crop."

"I guess the old folks just don't care," David said.

"Maybe you're right." Mr. Crayton was silent while he speeded up to pass a slow-moving truck. "Maybe you're right, but then again, maybe it's because they don't understand. You can't make folks understand something just by telling them. Take contour plowing, for instance. Ever since I've been at the training school, I've been talking it and demonstrating. The farm agent's been doing the same thing. It's just now catching on. It took years of telling and even showing to make them understand the losses they were taking. A little loss here and a little loss there mounts up. It's the same with what the young ones are missing in school."

In assembly that morning the principal talked about the same thing. About half the students in the high school department were absent. David heard what Mr. Jackson said, but it did not apply to him or to the others who were present. Most of those who were in their seats lived in town or, like Elizabeth Manning, on farms that were owned by their parents. Those who were absent were members of the poorer families, tenants who worked the land for a share of the crop. It seemed that tenants were always in debt, borrowing from the landowners for most of the year and "tot'ing up" in October or November when the crop was sold. A sharecropper considered himself fortunate if his share of the cash return enabled him to repay the owner. Then the cycle started all over again, drawing for store-bought food and winter clothing, and in the spring drawing again for seeds and fertilizer and supplies.

Maybe they didn't care. Anyway, they said little about it.

David saw that Ben Crawford was not there. Ben's father had once owned his land, but during the hard years when prices were low, he had gotten deep in debt and mortgaged his farm to Mr. Boyd. Later Boyd had foreclosed, but the Crawford family had been allowed to work the land for half the crop. This year Crawford was working in the city and trying to save money to buy the farm again. He had taken some days off so he could stay on the farm to get the seed beds started; then he had gone back to his job and left his family to carry on.

David decided he would walk from his home to Ben's after school and work with him in the field.

Through the day he missed Ben. They had grown up together, and they had a lot of fun. Ben claimed to be stronger than David, although he was not as tall. He took great pride in his muscular body and boasted of the hard work he could do. In school he tried hard, and David helped him; but he was often absent, and he had little time to do homework.

Ben's mother was a hardy woman who was used to the farm. She had learned little more than reading and writing in school, and though she often said she wished she had more learning, she added that she didn't know what she would do with it if she had it. On the farm with her, and equally able, was Velvet, the wife of Israel Crawford, Jr. Israel, Jr., had lost his right arm in Korea. He had returned home a bitter, silent man, clumsy and unable to do much of the farm work. Israel was away; it was something to do with his veteran's insurance. Israel said he might as well be away, for all the good he could do. Ben's baby sister, Sarah, was the only other helper at home. She was a little kid, only eight years old, but she could work.

That afternoon the sun was still high when David got started in the field with Ben and the others. He bent over with his feet set wide astraddle the row. With his right hand he shoved a wooden peg into the dirt, withdrew it to leave an even hole. The peg was transferred to the other hand, and from the basket on his left arm he took a soft young plant and set its root into the hole. He pressed the loose dirt around the plant, patted it down, and took a step forward in the yielding sandy soil. Another hole, another plant, another step. At first he was awkward. Those around him worked faster, their movements an easy rhythm. There was little talk. There was no laughter. This was work. It had to be done right. It had to be done fast. It had to be done.

David finished a row and straightened himself before he turned up the other side. His spacing had not been good. Plants set too close would not receive enough sunlight, and those too far apart wasted space between. As he bent again, he felt the sun hot on his back, but he liked it. Sunshine made you strong, they said. A hole, a plant, a step! If he could make each step the same length, his spacing would be even. Ben's little sister, Sarah, came abreast of him on a parallel row. She moved like a machine. David tried to keep up with her pace, but it was too much for him. Sarah turned her face and laughed as she saw him drop behind.

"Anyway," he thought, "give me a couple of days at this and a kid won't beat me."

At the end of his row this time he crossed over and started back with a single step, not stopping to straighten up. That was the way the others did it.

Velvet, tall and thin when she stood, seemed unhurried, but her hands moved swiftly, and one step was not finished before the next was started. Mrs. Crawford was short and fat, but her size did not slow her up. Her squat figure stomped up the row. With each step she seemed to plant herself for one short moment; with a jerk of the other side, she planted again. At the rate they were going, it would take no more than three days to finish the planting.

Three days out of school for Ben and Sarah! David remembered Mr. Crayton's words, "A little loss here and a little loss there mounts up."

It was like setting out plants that would not take root and grow up straight and full. They might be there, but they would not add their full share to the crop. If there were too many like that, the work would not be worth while. Too many days absent from school made the days present worthless. The student failed, once, maybe twice, and after that he dropped out.

After planting season, the fight against weeds and grass would start. Then they would work Saturdays and after school hours cutting out the extra growth with hoes and hilling up the soil around the plants. If grass and weeds got ahead too fast, they would stay out of school to catch up.

In the late afternoon Mrs. Crawford went to the house to cook supper, and Ben asked David to stop setting out and start watering, coming down the rows with a bucket and splashing each plant. David didn't mind the change. His back was getting sore anyway, and with watering he did not show up as slower than little Sarah and the others.

"It's a good day's work," Ben said, as they set off together for the house. "Sure enough we may get some rain tonight. Then if it's clear tomorrow, it'll make it just about perfect." The Crawfords' house was larger than the Williamses', but it looked less inviting. In the gathering dusk there was no evidence that it had ever been painted. The sides were weathered to the same drab earth gray as the roof. The only bright spots were Mrs. Crawford's flowers along the fence around the small front yard.

"You all hurry up and get washed," Mrs. Crawford called from the kitchen door. "Supper's ready."

It was dark when they gathered around the kitchen table to eat.

"Hope you can make out without electric, David," Velvet said.

"Well, it don't matter, I guess," David answered. It made him feel sort of ashamed to have Velvet talk as though he might mind. "A lot of folks didn't get the wires in on the first time around. You'll be getting yours before long."

"Humph! It's that Mr. Boyd," Velvet said. "He don't believe in government electricity for none of his tenants. Says it makes colored folks lazy."

"Ain't worth while to pass blame," Mrs. Crawford cut in as she forked a slice of salt meat out of the dish of boiled beans. "If we ever gets deed papers on this land again, we going fight to make it free and clear, and if shove-em-come-push anyhow, we ain't never going make mortgage."

"That's a big if." Velvet seemed to have little hope.

"'Tain't too big, though." Ben stood up to make his point. "If Israel hadn't gone in the army, we'd have made it before now."

"That's another if," argued Velvet. "If he'd had any sense, he never would have gone. Other farm boys got 'xempted. Israel always was dumb."

"Hush your mouth, gal!" Mrs. Crawford was angry.

"Israel knowed his rights. He didn't want to hold back. He's a full man, and he ain't no coward. If he ain't as fast talking as some, it's 'cause he thinks. He knows what he's doing."

"Hope someone around here knows what he's doing," Velvet said. She looked at Ben and David. "You so bright, going to high school and all."

David had heard that Velvet had made a good start in school, but her folks were sharecroppers, and they had kept her at home to help. Maybe she would have been different if she had gone on. She might have become a schoolteacher by this time. Now she was just another farm woman, rawboned and slovenly and kind of mean.

The next day and the next after that, David worked after school with the Crawfords. At home Ma and Betty Jane took care of the evening work. Ma said they didn't mind, but Betty Jane complained that David worked harder on other people's land than he would on their own.

It rained some, but only in showers, and on the third day they saw the section nearly covered. The plants they had set on the first day were struggling to stand up by themselves. David and the Crawfords were working at top speed when the sun went down. The soft dark crept around them, but they kept on with only a little rim of moon to give them light. Mrs. Crawford said the plants would grow well with the filling moon.

At supper that night Ben said he was going to be in school the next day. Sarah said she was going to sleep all day, just rest herself and sleep. Velvet was complaining about her back.

She could not stand straight from the ache of constant bending. Mrs. Crawford said nothing about how she felt, but David knew she must be mighty tired. His own back was hurting from the unaccustomed bending.

As he turned from the Crawfords' path into the unpaved road, David saw someone walking ahead of him. At first he thought it was an old man. He was walking slowly. Perhaps it was someone he knew. Though he was in a hurry to get home, David decided that if it was a colored man, he would slow up and walk with him.

When he got closer he could see that the man was not old, but he was limping and using a cane. David slacked his pace, hesitating to pass.

"Hi, fella!" the man said cheerfully, looking back. He was white. "How much farther is it to the highway?" He stumbled on a rough place and cursed the road, cursed himself, cursed his slow foot. It was all in the same cheerful voice, as though he really was not greatly disturbed, just talking as he naturally liked to talk.

"'Tain't far," David said. "Just about a mile."

"Yeah, one of them South Town miles, I bet!" The man laughed. "I remember."

The white man seemed to want to talk. It looked like he wanted company.

"Well, they say it's a mile from the highway to the Crawford place," David said.

The man turned and looked hard at David. "You ain't one of the Crawfords?"

"No, I'm David Williams. I live down the highway toward town."

"I used to know Israel Crawford," the man said. "Is he home now?"

"He's been home, but he had to go away again. I guess he'll be back soon," David said. "Israel lost an arm when he was in the army."

The man looked down at his leg.

"I been in the army," he said. "Been in veterans' hospital longer than that. Seems like I been in and out of hospitals half my life."

He slowed a bit to take out a cigaret, offering David one before he stopped to light up. As the match flared, David looked at his face. It was not familiar. But he figured the man must not be a stranger in South Town, even though he didn't know who he was.

They were coming up a long hill. Near the top the crippled man gave more attention to his steps. He talked less, and when he spoke it was as though he were alone — the bumpy road, the long hill, the slow foot. At the top of the rise, he started talking to David again.

"South Town! Pocahontas County! Home! I always thought I'd be glad to get back. God, how we used to talk about home! But I'd forgot how it was mostly. Never knew how hard folks can work and still stay poor. Never thought about being poor, even."

He said his folks were tenants, poor as rats, working other folks' land as long as he could remember.

As they came over the hill David pointed to the lights of cars passing on the highway below them.

The man cursed again. “Another mile!” he said. “I got to take five.”

He moved to the side of the road and eased himself down to sit with one foot in the ditch, the other straight out before him.

“Maybe you shouldn’t be walking on that bad leg,” David said.

“Got to get used to it,” the soldier replied.

David wondered if he had been wounded, but he had heard that veterans didn’t like to be asked about their injuries.

The soldier tapped his cane on the foot.

“Artificial,” he said. “They say you get used to ’em, but don’t let nobody fool you, boy. There ain’t nothing in the world that can take the place of the parts God gave you. Better take care of ’em.”

He smoked a while in silence, tossed off his cigaret and lit a fresh one.

“It was a colored fellow pulled me out that day in Korea. Took me out of the line of fire and went out again to get others that was down. The guy never come back.”

David wished he would go on. What was the battle like? Where was it, Heartbreak Ridge? Hillside? Jungle?

“I get to thinking about it sometimes.” The soldier went on, “They had a lot of colored hospital corpsmen. We saw ’em some on the transport. I never paid much attention, just colored fellows, just like the ones I seen around South Town or anywheres else. Some of 'em I guess had pretty good learning, 'cause they had lots of records to keep, and they knew their first-aid med care. Nobody thought much about 'em. But out there the old vets coming back told us. We just laughed, but after we got there we knew. Those black boys with their stretchers looked like angels. Only they wasn't angels, 'cause they got it the same as anybody else when the time came."

The man moved his bad foot to ease it, puffing on his cigaret.

"So Israel Crawford lost an arm," he said. "We used to fight when we were little, not hard, you know how it is. Us kids figured we didn't want colored boys around where we was. Guess they figured the same way about us."

The man laughed. "People are all kinds of fools. I don't suppose I was ever so glad to see anyone in my life as I was to see that colored fellow that helped me in Korea. It makes me mad now when I see colored folks put off in the Jim Crow car and stuff like that."

He started moving to get to his feet, cursing again with the pain, but still cheerfully. David gave him a hand, and as they walked together down the hill, the man held on. He needed the help. David was sorry he hadn't offered to help him sooner.

At the foot of the hill, where the road spilled into the highway, the man turned toward David. He looked hard. David felt that the man was looking right through his skin into where every man was the same.

"I remember you now," he said. "Your old man is Ed Williams, works at the Ford agency."

"That's right."

"My name's Travis, Solomon Travis." He put out his hand. "I'm flagging the bus here. I'm going to have me some fun. I'm going to ride in the back, in the Jim Crow seats," he laughed, "with the angels."

7

By the middle of May it was very hot.

It was a Friday afternoon. David was supposed to be concentrating on the decline of the Roman Empire. Mrs. Booker had asked questions which nobody could answer. She was trying very hard to explain the three reasons, but it was hot. Windows were open, and big noisy spring flies were going in and out. Across the highway David could see the pattern of brown rows curving with the hill in sharp contrast to the bright green of a field of new rye. Cows grazed in a meadow. Cars rolled by on Route One. A mule-drawn wagon passed. On the lowered tail-gate two boys sat with their feet swinging. They waved at the school, knowing that some would be watching them with envy.

Beyond the hill, treetops showed in dark silhouette. David thought of the old mill out there. It would be cool by the mill. The water would be chilly the first time you plunged in, but it would feel good to have a swim.

He wrote on his tablet in large letters, "Swim tomorrow?" and held it up for Ben Crawford to see. Ben nodded.

After school was dismissed, their plans were made. On Saturday morning David hustled through his work at home. At noon Ben came by, and the two boys talked loudly about the baseball game to be played back of the school that afternoon. They did not say they were going to South Town to play ball, but they talked about it and made sure that Mrs. Williams heard them.

It was hot again, hot while they walked, turning off Route One before they reached the school and taking the cut-off toward Bradley until they got to the little white church, where they turned again and followed the dirt road downhill toward the millpond.

"It's funny," Ben said, as they started taking off their clothes. "When you want to go swimming, it's so hot you think you can't stand it. Then when you get to the water, it seems right chilly."

"Yeah," David replied. "And when you first hit the water, oh, boy! Cold enough to freeze the ears off a brass monkey."

"Did you ever go in the old mill?" Ben asked. "Spooky old place, ain't it? I bet gangsters hide out in there sometimes. Nobody ever comes around."

They turned and looked at the abandoned mill for which

the stream had been dammed. Not a pane of glass in the windows remained unbroken. The roof was falling in. The dam still held, but the chute was broken, and the great water wheel no longer turned. Moss and vines and young sapling trees were holding it fast.

At the upper part of the pond, the end away from the dam, the water was not so deep. There was a stretch of clean gravel on the bank. They called it the beach.

"Good thing no women come down here," said Ben, kicking out of his shorts.

"Remember last year when those girls came and everybody had to stay in the water?" David asked, laughing at the memory.

"Yeah, they thought they were so smart!" Ben said. "But we fixed them. They lit out when we said we were all coming out just as we were, raw."

David put his foot into the water.

"Man, it's cold!" he said.

They debated the best way to go in. Farther downstream it was deep enough to dive from the bank, but the swiftness of the water as it poured over the dam made it too dangerous to go in there. In summer the water went over the dam in just a thin sheet. Now, so early in the season, the stream was swollen. There was a great rush. It seemed there must be two or three feet of water pouring over.

They got well back from the water and, each holding tightly to the hand of the other, they came down running fast and on into the water until they fell. It was as they knew it would be. At first the water chilled their skins, and then as they thrashed about, they got used to it. They swam across, using a crude overhand crawl stroke.

Both the boys were good swimmers. They had never been coached, and the form would have been considered bad among trained swimmers; but they did not know it, and they were happy. They made it across and swam back without stopping. When they came out, they were several yards farther downstream than where they had gone in.

"That current was sure pulling us," David said. "We got to be careful."

"We're far enough away from the dam," said Ben. "You just got to swim kind of upstream and you'll stay in line."

"I read about a guy going over Niagara Falls in a barrel." David went on to describe the attempt. Niagara, he said, was nearly a mile high. In the pool below the falls, friends were waiting with motor boats. They got the barrel, but when they opened it, the man inside was dead.

"Smothered, he was. No bones broken, but he was smothered."

"He must have been crazy," Ben said.

"Not crazy. He just wanted to take a chance," David argued.

"Anybody that takes fools' chances must be crazy," said Ben. "What's the good of it? What does he get if he lives? Crazy as a bedbug!"

While they lay in the warm sun, on their stomachs and then on their backs, to get tanned, as they said, they argued on the merits of taking chances. The talk went to war and fighting.

"Now you take in the army," Ben said, sitting up and leaning on one arm. "In the army a man's got to take chances, but he's doing it for a reason. If he dies, well, maybe he saves the others or he makes his side stronger."

"That's all right too," David argued back, "but just the same, he's just as dead as the guy smothered in the barrel. The guy in the barrel was trying to prove something. If he could do it, somebody else could."

"So what?" Ben had to laugh. It seemed so clear to him. "All he proved was that it couldn't be done."

"All right then." David thought he had made his point. "The guy proved it couldn't be done, not like that, anyway. So now nobody has to try the same thing. Next time they'll do it different."

"Okay, okay, next time they'll do it different. Now you go try it the different way. Maybe you'll prove that it can't be done your way, either."

"Well, now, look." David sat up and pointed toward the lower end of the millpond. "Suppose somebody you knew had gone over the dam and lived to tell about it. Suppose he told you just what he did and how he managed to save himself. I guess that information might be a lot of help to you."

"Aw, you're crazy!" Ben said. "A man wouldn't have a Chinaman's chance going over the dam. You can try it if you want to, and I'll be down below to haul out the remains —

if any. Just be sure to tell me what to say to your folks, that's all."

"But if you had to, what would you do?" David asked. "Let's go look at it."

The two boys rose and walked down along the bank. Near the dam they had to talk loudly, and when they had worked their way down to stand beside the pool below the waterfall, they had to shout to make themselves heard above the steady roar. They argued and they pointed, and they finally agreed that a person would probably be killed on such a trip.

As they came away they were both a little awed by the thought of what would happen to anyone who got swept over the dam. They did not speak until they got back to their beach.

"Just one thing a person might do," David said. "If I got caught in it, I would head upstream so I would go over feet first. Just as I reached the dam, I'd take in all the air my lungs would hold. When I went down, I would relax — you know, just go limp. And I'd pray, too."

"Yeah, you'd need to pray, I guess." Ben too was solemn at the thought. "Let's cross over again, and this time we'll keep swimming upstream."

Swimming easily and heading upstream, they were nearly halfway over when they heard someone call them from the bank. Looking back between strokes, they saw that others had come to swim. They were white boys.

Between the white and colored boys of South Town there was little conflict. Seldom was there a fight or even an argument between David's friends and any of the white boys.

David had heard that in some southern communities a constant state of feud was maintained. In South Town the white boys and the colored did not mix; they just stayed away from each other. They attended separate schools. They seldom talked together. That was the way David had grown up, and he thought little about whether it was good or bad. White boys of his age seemed to accept the condition in the same way David and his friends did.

If colored boys came to the millpond and white boys were swimming, the colored boys would take off their clothes and go in. Nobody objected, but the white boys would soon leave. If colored boys were in the water when the white boys came, they would start swimming and the colored boys would leave. They had no argument about it. There was no discussion.

"How's the water?" a white boy on the shore would call out to one of the colored boys in the water.

"Okay, I guess. Kind of cold."

Just small bits of communication, a bare exchange of words to show there was no ill will.

But David thought that some of the white boys were really mean. They acted bossy, as though they felt already that they were rich landowners and that the colored boys were poor tenants who owed them money.

Harold Boyd was the one whom David disliked most. Most of the white boys who followed him were as poor as David's friends, but they accepted his leadership because he had his own car and he always had money to spend.

When David and Ben reached the far bank this time, they went ashore and sat down to rest. Across the stream they saw Harold Boyd and four others. The smallest they recognized as Little Red, Harold's cousin. The tallest was Skinny Sattisfield. Skinny was over six feet tall and still growing.

Harold cupped his hands and hollered across the water, "You all come on out now! We want to swim!"

"Come on in, if you want to," Ben shouted back. "Ain't nobody stopping you!"

They had been about ready to go home, but they did not like to be told that they had to leave, especially by Harold Boyd. The fact that there were five of the others did not bother them. They had no thought of a fight. It was clear that Harold was just trying to be bossy. The boys with him started undressing.

To avoid looking like they were going to hurry, David and Ben walked up higher on the bank to sit on the grass in the sun.

"Gosh!" Ben said. "Funny how really white they look under their clothes."

"Yeah," David agreed. "White folks ought not go swimming without some kind of clothes. They sure look naked. Come on, let's go."

They waded in. On the bank opposite, Harold was arguing with his friends. He had not undressed.

Again they headed upstream so they would come out at the beach. They swam with slow, even strokes, keeping close together. When they came to shallow water and got their feet under them on the gravelly bottom, the others were still watching them. As they came out of the water Harold asked, "You all through now?"

"Well, I can't say," Ben replied. "We been having fun, and we might be going in again."

"Sure," David added, throwing himself down to lie in the sun. "There's plenty room. I wouldn't like bumping into you out there any more than you'd like bumping into me, but there's plenty room."

"Well, go ahead then, and hurry up," Harold said.

David lifted himself to look at Ben beside him. "You heard what the man said, Ben. He wants you to hurry up."

Ben put a surprised look on his face. "Yes, Dave," he said. "I'm hurrying. Just watch me." He lay on his back and put his hands under his head. One leg crossed the other. "Watch me hurry, Dave." He closed his eyes and pretended to be asleep.

"Aw, come on, Harold," Skinny Sattisfield said. "They ain't no trouble. Let's go in."

"I don't associate with —" Harold paused as David raised his head to look at him. "I don't socialize with field hands," he said.

They walked a few paces along the bank going toward the dam. There was more talk, with Harold holding out and the others trying to make him see that no harm would be done even if all were in the water at the same time.

"All right," the self-appointed leader said loudly, "but they'd better not come in while I'm in there."

The others did not enter the water at the little strip called the beach. They were downstream. The bank was steeper there. It was also nearer the dam.

David did not like that. He was sorry. Maybe he shouldn't have bucked against Harold Boyd. Well, it was Harold's fault. He had spoiled his own fun.

David raised up and looked at the boys standing waist deep. They had not swum out into the stream.

"Hey, fellows," he called to them, trying to keep his voice friendly, "the current's awful swift down there, and it's deep. Come on up this way."

"You mind your own business," Harold called.

Ben turned over and said, "Come on, let's go. We had our fun."

David agreed. They had had their fun. They had stayed around long enough to show that they could not be chased. "Okay," he said, and they started for their pile of clothes.

Ben was dressed, and David was sitting on the ground putting on his shoes when the others started to swim across. All of them seemed to be good swimmers. They were heading upstream to avoid the pull of the current. It was a long way down to the dam, but there was a strong current, and they had to deal with it.

"David, look at that," Ben said. "They're taking an awful chance."

David got to his feet to see better.

"Yes," he said, "that's dangerous. Little Red is a good swimmer, but he's stroking too fast. He'll get tired."

They were less than halfway across when Skinny Sattisfield called out to the others. He turned and started back. Another boy was abreast of the redhead. Little Red was not pulling so fast now.

David cupped his hands and called out, "Hey, you fellows. You ain't halfway, you better turn back."

The boy in the lead slowed down and trod water while he looked around. He said something to Little Red, but Red kept on. The boy who had stopped started swimming again, and he was soon up to Red.

Harold turned and started back.

The other, who was the slowest swimmer, turned.

"Gosh!" David exclaimed. "Red is game all right. He's just about halfway now. He's got to swim, though. They're both going downstream fast."

Those who had started back were being drawn by the current too. They were now trying only to reach the shore. They were tired.

The boy in the lead was far ahead of Little Red now. He would make it. He was still going strong with long, even sweeps. Red slowed down. He trod water for a moment, and while he slowed, it was plain that the current in midstream was pulling him.

Ben called, "Go on, Red! Go on! You can make it."

But Red looked back. He tried to measure the distance from shore to shore, and he turned and started back.

"The other way, Red," David called, motioning with his arms. "You're closer to the other side! Go on! Go on!"

The boy was confused. He started pulling faster. He couldn't keep up at that rate. For a while he made progress. He was pulling with all his might. David and Ben moved down along the bank.

"God help him," David said. "The current's carrying him too fast. He's getting panicky. If he could keep pulling. . . . Ben, the kid won't make it."

He kicked off his shoes and shucked out of his pants and shirt.

Ben grabbed his arm.

"You can't do it, Dave," he shouted. "You can't help him. You'll both go over."

David was breathing hard as he kept his eyes on the redhead. He was still pulling, but there was little strength in his arms. He was less than half the stream's width away.

"I got to try. I got to try!" He took one look at the dam, still two hundred yards away.

"Good luck, Davie boy!" Ben said as David dived, getting all the gain he could from the plunge.

Near the shore the current was not too strong. Beyond where Little Red was, the water would be running more swiftly. David figured that if he kept swimming straight from shore the current would carry him downstream just about as fast as it was taking Red. He would have to keep going to reach the kid before he was swept over. Maybe he could help the younger boy to reach the shore, but it was a lot to hope for. Most likely they would go over together. This plan he and Ben talked about, maybe it would work.

As he raised his arm from the water, he looked back and saw Ben helping one of the boys up the bank. Ben would know what to do. It was good they had talked about it. Ben would be at the foot of the dam. Now he could hear the roar of the water, and there was Red's face ahead of him.

"Hi, Red!" He smiled, but the younger boy was too exhausted to smile back; maybe he was scared too. David turned beside Red. "Put your hand on my shoulder and rest yourself. That's it. I got you. Take it easy now. We'll be all right, Red."

David set himself a slow breast stroke. He found he was tired too. His words had come in gasps. When he spoke again, he tried to make his voice sound easy.

"We can make it, Red. Ben and the others will be on the other side to help us. Take deep breaths now. Loosen up all you can. We're heading upstream so we go over feet first. You don't get hurt that way. Just before we go over, you take a deep breath and hold it, but let your body go loose. On the other side you can swim again. The fellows will be there. Get it?"

There was no spoken answer, but David felt Red's hand on his left shoulder tighten. It was more than a pat on the shoulder; it was like a handshake. He turned and looked into Little Red's eyes, and Red's face broke into a smile.

The last thing David remembered before he went over was Little Red's smile. He noticed, too, that the boy's hair was not really red when it was wet and that his skin was not really white.

This is it!

He was falling, falling, falling.

There was a sudden shock to his whole body, and then everything was dark. He was still falling, and in the darkness there was light. Falling gently, and the lights were dimmer. Falling. Falling. Falling.

Some time later it seemed that he was drifting. Just drifting in space, and then he was a little higher. He was drifting upwards. Far away a familiar kindly voice was saying the same words over and over, but far away in another world, a long time ago in another age. He felt himself being lifted gently upward. The voice went on. The light, the beautiful lights in the darkness. Floating upward. The words, "Place, Pressure, Release . . . Place, Pressure, Release." If he could move. If he could move only so much as a finger. He had no control. He tried again, thinking hard about it. His finger twitched, and then he knew someone had spoken his name.

It was all right.

He smiled.

8

When it got around that David Williams had saved the life of Mr. Boyd's nephew, everybody said that Mrs. Williams should be very proud to have such a son. If she was proud, she did not show it. She cried and held her son close to her. David felt that his mother was watching him as though he had been away and had come back as a stranger.

Dr. Anderson came to the house early in the evening that same day. He had been called to the Boyds' to see about Harold and Little Red. Mr. Boyd sent him to see David.

All the colored people loved old Dr. Anderson. They said he was one white man in whose heart there was no race prejudice. He had said openly that he was not a skin specialist interested in color and that under the skin there were no race problems. Really he was not so old, but he was stooped, and bald with a fringe of white hair — and he was very gentle.

David's right knee was cut, and his shoulder on the same side was swollen and sore. The doctor approved of the way Mrs. Williams had washed the cut with a lysol solution and applied a dressing with carbolated Vaseline. He showed more concern for the painful shoulder, and after his examination, he ordered David to stay in bed for a day or so.

He sat a long time with David and with Ben, who had stayed around to do David's work. Mrs. Williams stood in the door listening and following every detail of what she heard.

Ben told what he had done.

"After Dave started, I knew he would be going over with Red," he said, "and I knew I'd need all the help I could get down below the dam. When the others came out of the water, they were pretty beat. Harold was the worst. Gosh! You should have seen him when he knew Red was still out there. He was mad. He wanted to fight. I had a hard time getting him quiet." Ben stopped and shook his head.

"Well, Skinny Sattisfield and one of the others went with me," he went on. "I got out of my clothes, and the three of us stood and watched where the water was coming over. It sure seemed like a long time, and the water looked just like a big hunk of solid glass — green it was, with the light shining through it. Then they came, David and Red side by side. I went in and came up with Red. He was out, but he was breathing. Then we couldn't find Dave. Boy, was I scared! I started running down the bank; then Skinny hollered, and I saw him dive. He got Dave, and we hauled him out on the bank, and I started giving artificial respiration."

Dr. Anderson looked his surprise, so Ben explained. "We used to practice artificial respiration and the other things in first aid. David always was the best at that stuff, but this was the real thing, and Dave was the victim. I guess I figured I had to do it right. But I was scared, and Dave was sure a long time coming around."

"Where was Harold Boyd all this time?" the doctor asked.

Ben smiled.

"Harold seemed to go clean out of his head just after he came out of the water. He thought Little Red was gone for sure, and he just about went crazy," Ben said. "We had to leave him up on the bank. I had to use a little forcible persuasion."

"You hit him?" asked David.

"I had to. I had to knock him out." Ben added quickly, "It didn't hurt him, though. He didn't even remember afterwards. And he drove us all home in his convertible.

"Harold talked different coming home," Ben said. "He told us what happened was his fault. Said you warned them about swimming where the current was so strong and he told you to mind your own business. I guess Harold kept thinking how he nearly got Red drowned.

"Boy," Ben went on, "is that convertible of Harold's nice! Never thought I'd get a ride in that car, him always acting so mean and all."

"Why do you suppose he acts like that?" David asked.

"Someone like that, that's got everything, you think he'd act nice."

"It's his family," David's mother said. "A man like you, Dr. Anderson, you would never know how mean a woman like Mrs. Boyd can be."

"I do know," Dr. Anderson said. He looked sad. "Mr. and Mrs. Boyd are hard people. The worst part of it is that people like them believe they are right. They've always been taught that God ordained that colored people should be servants and helpers, 'hewers of wood and drawers of water.' They really believe that Negroes are inferior people, unable to think or plan or understand."

Dr. Anderson went on talking. He talked in a soft voice as if he were thinking out loud. He said there were lots of people like the Boyds — in the South and in the North and everywhere in the world. People who believe things because that's what their parents thought and their grandparents, and people farther back. Their minds are closed to new ideas. But the world is full of new ideas — and they won't down. Some of the ideas weren't really new at all, but it had taken a long time for the masses of people to think they were even possible. Millions and millions of people all over the world had nothing; their parents and grandparents before them had nothing. That was the way things were, and the people didn't expect anything.

But things are changing. People travel more and see more, and there is a wider communication of ideas. People everywhere are thinking that maybe some day there can be enough food for everyone, and decent homes, and education for everyone — as much as anyone wants.

"And maybe education comes first," Dr. Anderson said. "With education and understanding, maybe people everywhere can have a better life. Maybe with more education for both white and colored people, they can learn to live together.

"It has to happen," the doctor said. "Because the world itself is in trouble. If we don't, colored and whites together, stop fighting each other, we'll all be over the dam and lost."

Mrs. Williams thought of when her own son was about to go over a dam and perhaps be lost. Ben had told her how David had planned just what he would do if he should get caught in the stream and washed toward the dam.

"You were praying out there," she said to David. Her voice showed the strain of deep feeling. "You were praying just before you went over, weren't you, Son?"

David snapped his fingers.

"Gosh! That's what I forgot!" he said. "I clean forgot to pray just then."

The doctor laughed, and Ma looked hurt.

"I was praying for him, though," Ben said quickly. "I was sure praying while he was in there."

"You know," David said, "I should have prayed. I really was scared at first. I didn't know what I ought to try to do, but by the time I got to Little Red and started talking to him, I wasn't scared any more. I just felt sure that it was going to be all right and . . . well, I know I should have, but I just didn't feel any need for praying when the time came."

Dr. Anderson turned to Mrs. Williams.

"When the time came," he said softly, "the prayers were already answered."

All through the following day, which was Sunday, people were coming in, white people along with colored. The white people spoke about what a fine house it was. They admired the house and the furniture as much as they admired David. After what Dr. Anderson had said, David and Ben got a laugh out of the sight of colored and white people mingling in the home of a Negro.

Mr. and Mrs. Boyd came with Harold. Mr. Boyd was a large man. He seemed to crowd the little room, and his voice boomed. Mrs. Boyd brought a cake and some home-made ice cream. She stood by the bed, and she looked like she was going to cry. Harold looked very uncomfortable.

For the summer David was promised a job at Mr. Boyd's Ford agency, where Ed Williams used to work.

"It's not a matter of money, boy," Mr. Boyd said. "I'm not trying to pay you for what you did, but I want you to have a chance to learn, and I'm willing to take you on. You can make good if you pay attention to your work and be respectful."

"That's what you'll have to do, boy," Mrs. Boyd added, "pay attention and be respectful. We appreciate what you did."

"Just the same," Mr. Boyd said, "you might as well understand that you'll be expected to stay in your place. These radical ideas going around are only going to make trouble for you people. Ed," he said, speaking to David's father, "why don't you come on back to your job and settle down to live with your family? They need you, and what little money you're making in the city and what goes with it is getting you so mixed up that you'd be better off without it."

"I'll think about it, Mr. Boyd," Williams said. David wished his father would say more, answer back. Williams repeated, "I'll think about it."

Harold stayed behind when the others left the room.

"I guess I can't tell you just how I feel," Harold said. His face was red, but his eyes met David's. "I think about how I'd be feeling if you hadn't gone in after Little Red — how we'd all be feeling."

He held out a canvas zipper bag. "I brought you something, David. It's my baseball suit and the spikes."

"Gosh!" David was surprised. He was surprised and pleased too at the change in Harold. "But you don't have to do that, Harold. You'll be wanting to play ball this summer."

"That's all right." Harold smiled, and his smile seemed right friendly. "I won't be needing it anyway. We're going down to Bacon's Beach for the summer, and they don't play ball much there, just swim and fish. You're right welcome if you can use it."

"Well, thanks a lot, Harold."

"I'm thanking you, David, for everything."

David felt silly staying in bed. After the Boyds left, he got up and tried on the baseball suit. The arm and shoulder were sore, but he managed. Betty admired him and told him he looked like a big leaguer and called him Jackie Robinson. His father had little to say, but he did not tell David to get back in bed; so David kept on the uniform until he went to bed at the usual time.

He lay thinking, happy at the prospect of a job, thankful for the suit Harold had given him, but wondering about the meaning of all that had been said.

He agreed that people should be respectful, but he did not believe that this was what the Boyds meant. He wished that his father had explained to Mr. Boyd that working in the city and making money on a regular job was better than staying in South Town to work for the low pay which Boyd offered to all his workers who were colored. He wished his father had said that colored people just want to work and live like anybody else, and that this is not a radical idea.

David wished his father had said it. Instead of speaking out, he had said he would think about coming home to stay. He did not speak his thoughts. Most colored people, when white people were about, did not speak their thoughts. With Dr. Anderson it was different. They had spoken freely with the doctor, but he was not like the others. What he had said seemed reasonable, and also he had listened. With him it was not necessary to be silent. Why, David asked himself, should colored people be so silent? Why did they not explain their thoughts? Somebody should tell the Boyds and the others like them just what the colored people were thinking, what they were hoping for and looking forward to. It seemed so simple to David, yet he recognized that perhaps most white people did not know. They did not understand colored people. They did not know, because no one had told them. Somebody should tell them. Colored people should tell them.

Maybe it would take educated colored people to make them understand. Ben's father had said a man would have to have education and guts.

If a colored man had enough education and good common sense, he ought to be able to make white people understand. He could speak out. He could make his voice ring out for his people. He wouldn't have to be especially brave, he would just have to know. Maybe that was what the lady who gave money for the paint had meant, about the school ringing out in the silences. Maybe it would be for him, David Williams, to speak out of the silences for his people. He would be their doctor, healing their bodies and understanding their problems, and he would be the one to speak for them.

Yes, he would do it. He would make the others understand. He would just explain and be reasonable. Not now, but some day he would be ready. He would speak out so well and so clearly that all the people, white and colored, would hear him, and they would understand.

He knew it would take a long time to get his education, but he pictured himself carrying his little black doctor's bag into the humble homes on the farms and in the towns of Pocahontas County. He would comfort the old people and always listen carefully when they described their ills and told about their many home remedies. He would joke with the children, and they would love him. People would tell him all their troubles, and he would help them overcome poverty and ignorance. He would organize the farmers and lead committees to the banks and to the government agencies, arranging for sharecroppers to buy small farms. Some day he would make an eloquent plea for better schools and houses and more of them and for better opportunities for all.

He was deeply moved by his sense of dedication. He pushed the covers away and sat up straight in the bed. He squared his shoulders, and he spoke the words: "The voice of David Williams ringing out in the silences!"

In all his life, he would never be able to forget this moment.

9

For the first few days on his new job at the South Town Ford Agency, David did only the work of a janitor. The small showroom and the offices had not been properly cleaned for a long time. David washed windows, glass show cases, and paint work. In the shop he removed accumulated scrap from under benches and scraped grease and washed walls and scrubbed floors. When everything was clean inside, Mr. Boyd sent him to clean up the lot back of the garage. The high grass had to be cut first.

Then he piled the old motor blocks together and arranged steel frames, shafts, and geared wheels in a semblance of order.

Mr. Boyd watched him closely. He did not say much.

He just told David what to do next, and sometimes he would say, "That looks better now," or "That's all right, boy."

David was glad that nothing was said about what he had done at the millpond. It was better to feel that Mr. Boyd was the boss rather than a kind man who was doing something for him out of gratitude. David worked hard, and on Saturdays when he received his pay, he could feel that he had earned the money.

One of those who welcomed him and tried to help him on the new job was Solomon Travis, the white veteran David had talked with early in the spring. Travis was working as a mechanic. He had learned to use his artificial leg so well that nobody would feel he was handicapped. He hardly limped when he walked.

After the second week, Mr. Boyd left David to take his orders from the shop superintendent, Mr. Mundy. David did a few wash jobs, and he helped to grease cars. He studied the charts and printed instructions and planned for the time when he would be allowed to work without close supervision.

One day David saw a shop manual on the work bench. Not being busy at the time, he turned the pages and started reading on engine lubrication.

"We all know you can read, boy," Mundy said as he came out of his office. "We know you been to school, but you don't have to worry about books here. You just do what we tell you, and you'll make out better."

"I was just reading about different grades of oil to use, Mr. Mundy," David said.

"Well, I'll tell you what you need to know." Mundy picked up the manual and turned toward his office.

"You put in Number 30 when we tell you to, and you put in Number 20 when we tell you to. If we don't tell you, then you ask. That's all you have to know."

Ed Williams said differently, however.

"It's all in the books," he told David as they sat on the steps at home Sunday morning. "They got books and charts for everything. You can understand them better than I could when I went there to work. Don't lose time on the job, but study some of these books I bought, and read those at the shop when you get the chance. The super ought to be glad to see you trying to improve yourself."

But Pa did not know Mundy. Pa's old super had left South Town. This new man was hard to please. He wasn't mean, exactly. He knew his job. He knew all the different kinds of cars that were brought in for repairs. When a late model expensive car came in, he did the work himself. He would let no one else touch it.

"Mr. Mundy's funny," David said. "He won't trust anybody. It's not just that he's white. He watches the white mechanics and bawls them out just like he does us. He keeps everything locked up, and whenever a man gets a tool he has to sign for it. Sometimes they lose more time waiting around for him to come back to issue a wrench than the old wrench is worth."

"Yeah, I know that kind," Ed Williams said.

"The others, especially the white mechanics," David went

on, "waste a lot of time that way. They say they don't care, because it's the super's fault."

"Well, don't you get into it," Pa warned. "You let the white folks fight it out between 'em. Do your own work, and don't lose time. You're working for Mr. Boyd."

"Oh, I keep right on. There's always plenty for me to do," David said. "They put a lot on me because I'm new. I don't mind it, though, not too much, except when they put something on me when I already have a job to do. Then Mr. Mundy bawls me out for not getting through."

"You ought to tell him," Pa said. "Don't let them put that kind of stuff over on you."

"He won't let you say anything," replied David. "He calls that talking back, and he gets mad."

"Well, you'll know what to do," said Pa, with an encouraging smile. "I know how it is when you're working on a job. You have to decide when to talk and what to say when the time comes. Just use your head, boy, use your head."

David used his head most of the time, and he got on well. Mr. Boyd saw little of him, and he seemed to approve what he did see. Mundy sometimes reprimanded him for being slow, but more often he would show him a better or faster way of doing the job.

Sam McGavock was the oldest and the most highly skilled mechanic on the job. He had worked there with David's father, and he took every opportunity to help the son of his friend. Besides McGavock and Travis, there were two other white mechanics. Joe Brodnax was a mechanic, but he was colored and did not get a mechanic's pay.

Joe was an old friend. He told David that his father used to teach him when he was just a helper. Now Joe was anxious to help David. Every day David ate his lunch with Joe.

The other helpers, white and colored, were careless boys who wanted David to join them in outwitting Mundy and getting out of work. After the first few days they agreed that David was different. They let him alone.

As the weeks went by, David worked on repair jobs more and more with the different mechanics. When he worked with Joe, they would talk about the families and friends they knew. Working with McGavock he learned a lot about the trade. Every job was a lesson, and old Mr. Mack, as the boys called him, was a careful teacher. David enjoyed most working with Travis, the veteran. He was not such a good mechanic, but he worked hard, putting a lot of energy into everything he did. He talked the same way, using strong language for emphasis.

One afternoon Travis got to talking about colored soldiers he had seen in Korea. He spoke of their courage and ability, saying that they were true Americans in the army although they were not recognized as such in civilian life.

"But there's going to be some changes made," he said, speaking loudly and punctuating his remarks with colorful oaths. "You'll see. Folks are learning what democracy and liberty mean. Colored and white can't work together or go to school or church together; they can't eat in the same restaurant together. We fought together. In the war we slept huddled up in the same holes. We drank the stinking water out of the same cups and smoked off the same butts when we had 'em.

"By God, if we can fight together and die together, we'd ought to be able to live together."

David had been thinking about the right to work and be paid like anybody else. He wasn't anxious about white and colored living together. He could hardly imagine going to school with white boys and girls. It hadn't come up seriously in his thoughts. He had heard colored people talk like this white man, but they were not the people who had always lived in Pocahontas County. Around South Town, colored people did not discuss social equality. It was among the thoughts hidden in the silences. David's father had advised keeping away from white people, not getting closer to them.

Mundy stood at his office door listening. Neither David nor the mechanic was idle. They were doing a clutch job. Travis was leaning into the car's open door with his back to the office. David was leaning from the other side. He could see Mundy. David asked a question about a bolt that was giving him trouble. The mechanic straightened up and gave a thrust to the wrench. Helped perhaps by the words he used, the bolt came free.

He dropped back to his own side and went on with the same line of talk.

"Take you now," he said. "Take yourself. You got savvy. You're catching on fast. When you learn the trade, you got a right to work the same as anybody else and get paid the same way, or go in business for yourself. That's what democracy means." Mundy had crossed the floor to stand behind Travis. "Look at Joe Brodnax now. He's a good mechanic, as good as any of us in here. Does he get paid for a mechanic? I ask you now, does he?"

"Travis, I want to see you in the office," Mundy said, tapping the mechanic's shoulder.

Travis looked up. "In the office?" he asked.

"Come on. Right away." Mundy turned and walked off.

"Okay, Sarge!" Travis said, with a grin. He started to show David how to go on while he was away.

"I said right away!" Mundy shouted at him.

"Well, I'm a monkey's uncle! Wonder what's the matter with the old buzzard." The veteran squared his shoulders and walked off with only the suggestion of stiffness in his left leg.

Loud and angry words came over the grill of the superintendent's office. There was no question in David's mind about what was being said on both sides. He knew. He remembered a song the people sometimes sang in church:

"They are fighting
They are fighting
Over me, over me,
And before I'll be a slave
I'll be buried in my grave
And go home to my Lord and be free."

It was an old song out of Civil War days when the

country was battling over the issue of slavery. On the plantations his people had gathered to pray and sing at night in their cabins. Messages had gone by word of mouth with news of battles — Gettysburg, Atlanta, the siege of Richmond, the battle of the ironclads. Men had fought and died to make emancipation a reality. It was all in the stories David had heard over and over.

He was losing time. He was not doing the work. He lifted his head and saw that no one else was working. Joe, the colored mechanic, was not in sight. The two colored helpers were gone. The white workers were just listening.

The door of the superintendent's office flew open. Mundy strode toward the front door leading to the business offices, and Travis followed him. Mundy was saying nothing, but Travis was shouting his defiance.

McGavock walked over to David.

"What's it all about, boy?" he asked.

"I don't exactly know, Mr. Mack," David said, without looking up. "We were talking here. He was saying some things about democracy and what they had been fighting for. Then the super came and called him into the office."

McGavock looked hard at David. He had always felt free to say things to Ed Williams that white men seldom said to colored.

"Talking about democracy," he repeated. "I get it. I fought for democracy in France, too, but you can't talk about it here." He went back to his bench and took up a ball peen hammer and stood tapping on a vise.

David leaned into the car. The lower edge of the door cut into his thighs. The smell of rancid engine oil filled his nostrils. The steady *tap tap tap* of McGavock's hammer and the undertones of argument in the front office reached his ears. It was hot and close. A lump stuck in his throat. His mouth was dry. He felt sick at his stomach, and he had to take himself away and go to the colored toilet. He vomited.

When he came out, Travis was packing his tools.

Mr. Boyd was standing in the front door. McGavock still stood tapping on his vise. None of the colored workers had returned.

David expected Mr. Boyd to call him and fire him too, but he had to speak to Travis.

"I'm sorry, Mr. Travis," he said.

Travis stopped wiping his tools to look at him.

"Sorry for what? You got nothing to be sorry about," he said. "Neither have I, not a thing, not a blessed thing! These dumb fools. They'd rather die than do the right thing. For me, I don't care. I'd rather die too than be like them."

Travis went on wiping his tools and putting them into the box.

"One thing," he went on. "They can't make me over. They can't make me think like they do, and they can't make me keep still, either. I'm American. I got freedom of speech; and you're American too, Dave — don't ever forget that."

Travis snapped his box shut and turned to put out his hand.

"Good luck, fellow!" he said. "Don't be sorry. I'm the

one that's sorry. I wish I was black. I'd show them."

Very little work was done for the rest of the day.

David took off the clutch housing. Nobody gave him anything else to do. Mundy stayed in his office most of the time. Chief Peebles came and talked to Mundy. Before he left, the two of them stood in the door and watched David while he swept. They talked, but they said nothing to David. He was glad when six o'clock came and he could go home.

David was not discharged. Mr. Boyd's attitude toward him showed no change. The superintendent seemed to watch him more closely, but he never mentioned Travis's conversation.

"That was bad stuff," Joe said to David the next day while they were eating their lunch. "'Course us colored folks all know that what the white boy was saying is true. You know it, but you can't say it. Your pa worked in there, and he's a better mechanic than any of the white men, better than Mr. Mack. He wasn't never paid like them."

"I thought sure Mr. Boyd was going to fire me too," David said. "Maybe he will yet."

"Mr. Boyd's all right," Joe said. "He don't bother you so long as you stay humble. You ain't did nothing. Besides, you got the Indian sign on him."

"Well, maybe he does have some feeling for me," David said. "I wouldn't ask special favors, though. I wouldn't ask anything. I want to feel that I earn every dime he pays me."

"I wasn't talking about what you did at the millpond."

Joe laughed as he explained. "I mean your pa. Ed Williams is a good man. Old man Boyd expects he'll be coming back one of these days, and he don't want Ed to go off to work for the Chevvie people or over to Plymouth. Even if you wasn't no good to him at all, he'd want to keep a hold on your pa."

David had cause to remember Joe's words when Mr. Boyd spoke to him a few days later. His first duty at eight o'clock every morning was to sweep the offices and the showroom. His last duty in the evening was to sweep out the shop. Usually he was through with the offices before Mr. Boyd and the clerks came in. On this morning Mr. Boyd came early.

"How are you getting on, Dave?" he asked.

David said he was getting along fine. He thought he was learning a lot too.

"You'll be all right, boy, if you learn to keep your head. You come from good stock," Mr. Boyd said. "I've known Ed and your mammy a long time. Ed's a good boy too."

David went on with his dusting. He felt like asking how old a colored boy had to be before he was a man, but he didn't say anything. This wasn't one of the times.

"How's Ed doing down there in the city now?" Mr. Boyd went on without waiting for an answer. "I guess he'll be coming back looking for a job any day now. I hear things are tightening up. In the Ford organization, we're making our plans. You tell Ed I don't hold it against him for leaving me in the lurch. You tell him I'm willing to take him back when his city job folds up. Say, maybe he'd better come on in now, not wait until they close down. You tell him come see me, you hear?"

"Yes, sir," David said. "I'll tell him next time he comes home."

"Yeah, just tell him he'd better come on in now, while we can make a place for him." Mr. Boyd was sounding very easy about the whole thing. "Tell him I'll take him back."

10

Summer was going by all too swiftly.

On the fourth of July David went to Alberta to play ball with his team. He knocked out two home runs, and South Town came out winner twelve to five. After the game he swam, and then there was a dance at the schoolhouse. David didn't care much for dancing, but he went along, and he had fun.

It was a hot summer. The other helpers in the shop laid off from work for days at a time. A mechanic was hired to replace Travis, but he was not very good at the work. More cars were brought in for repairs than the shop could take. There was a brisk turnover in used cars. David was doing jobs that were usually given only to mechanics. The superintendent seemed to trust him as much as he dared trust anybody.

Ben's brother, Israel Crawford, Jr., was home again. Al Manning, who was only a few years older than David, was home, too, no longer a boy. Al walked and spoke as a hard man, somewhat like Travis. He talked to any who would listen. He talked about the things he had seen and the things he had done. He talked about things he wasn't going to take. He spoke of fighting back and of dying.

On his Sundays at home, Ed Williams was saying little about the future. David could see that his father was worried, and he told him that Mr. Boyd was willing to hire him again. He did not go to talk it over with Mr. Boyd.

Then one day Ed Williams brought his work clothes and his tools home. Contracts had been canceled, and thousands of workers had been let out. Pa said he was going to take a few days rest; besides, with David working every day, there were many things to be done around the place. Mr. Boyd told David to ask his father when he would be ready to go back into the shop. Williams said he wasn't sure. He wasn't just sure, but he would be in town one day soon to see about it.

"David," he said one evening, sitting on the front steps after supper, "David, I was trying to work out something, but it just didn't make. You sure you want to be a doctor?"

"That's what I'd like more than anything else, Pa," David replied. "They say it's a hard course. I talked some to Mr. Jackson and Dr. Anderson about it. They showed me it wouldn't be easy. But I think I'll make it some day."

"You'll make it, Son, some day." Pa shook his head. "I'm awful afraid that some day is getting pushed far off, and I don't like it any better than you do. I talked with some of the school people in the city. I never knew before what you were missing in the training school. I just didn't know. Nobody told me. The people here boast about it. I thought it was all right.

"Then I was hoping right up to the last that I could stay on at the plant." Pa was silent for a moment. Then he went on. "Way back in the spring I heard that a lot of men would be laid off soon. They said those working in the machine shop without much seniority would be among the first to go. Then I thought if I lost out in the machine shop, I could stay in the plant at some other job, doing anything — roustabout, cleaning, anything so long as it would give a chance to get the family, especially you, down there for school."

"Oh, the school's not so bad here." David saw that Pa was feeling low, blaming himself for what certainly was not his fault.

"I could have quit the factory and got a job in a garage," he said. "I'm a good mechanic. But after the layoffs started, a lot of men were out scrambling, white and colored. There were jobs, but they were only for old-timers in the city. They said for us to get out of town, go back to the farm, clear out."

David told his father that it would not matter. A little more time after graduating at South Town. Maybe an extra year. And folks were saying that with all the talk about the Supreme Court decision, the school would be improved.

Mr. Williams did not expect to see the improvement soon enough.

David saw that his father was spending a restless week at home. He worked all of every day around the house, at the barn, and in the garden. He spoke of getting running water and plumbing in the house. Ma said he had been spoiled by the modern plumbing.

It was clear he was holding back from going to see Mr. Boyd. At the breakfast table on Monday of his second week at home, Pa told David that he would be in town later. David knew he meant that he would be at the Ford agency.

At his work that morning David kept watching the door to the showroom, thinking that his father might come to the shop after talking with Mr. Boyd. In the middle of the morning he was putting a carburetor on a '51 Ford. It wasn't a new carburetor. It was one which he had cleaned and a mechanic had adjusted. Now it was being sold as a replacement. The carburetor he was taking off would undergo the same process.

He saw Mr. Boyd come into the showroom. He called Mundy, and they went together into the super's office. When they came out, David had finished his job and McGavock was adjusting the idling throttle. Mr. Boyd walked toward David.

"How long have you been here now, David?" he asked.

"Nearly three months, sir," David replied.

"Well, we're making some adjustments," Mr. Boyd said. "Maybe I made a mistake when you first came here to work. I can't keep on paying what I have been. You'll get an adjustment in your pay this week."

Mr. Boyd looked like he expected an argument, almost as if he was daring David to argue. Use your head, Pa had said.

"Well, you know, Mr. Boyd," David said, "I appreciate the chance to work for you, and I want to thank you kindly, but I've got to go back to school in a couple of weeks anyway." David was going to say that he understood the change of conditions and that for his remaining time he was willing to take the cut, but Mr. Boyd did not wait.

"Back to school?" He was excited, and he talked loud. "What are you going to school for? That's the trouble now. You people are getting too high-minded to stay in your place. You and your pappy too. What do you want to go to school for? You're busting out with smartness already."

David did not understand. Mr. Boyd had seemed to be a reasonable man. McGavock had moved away. Mundy had come closer.

"You know," David said, with his voice not nearly as full as he would have liked it, "I want to be a doctor."

"Doctor! Doctor!" Mr. Boyd's face was red, and the corners of his mouth turned down as though he tasted something unpleasant. "You look like a doctor." He looked David over from head to foot. Dirty, oil-stained, hands greasy. "I believe I had to warn you once before about your high-faluting ways. I had almost forgot that. I wanted to forget it." He came a step closer. "I ought to give you the thrashing of your life. Your pappy won't do it, and you need it." McGavock came back to the car. He was carrying a heavy wrench. "I won't soil my hands with you. You're a dirty, stinking black little ingrate. You get off my property, and if you or your pappy ever cross my path again, I'll kill you. Do you hear?"

David heard.

He had some things, some tools of his own, but he did not stop for them. As he turned toward the door to the alley at the side, he saw that Joe had been standing beside McGavock.

"Doctor!" He heard Boyd's voice behind him. "Keep that stinking black doctor off my property."

David might have gone around by Brown's restaurant and caught a ride toward his home. He didn't want to see anybody, though, so he started walking.

He could not understand what had gotten into Mr. Boyd. All the summer the man had been pretty decent. Being out of work was not bad. He had saved his money, and he was ready to quit, and Pa . . . what about Pa? . . . Mr. Boyd had said hard things about "your pappy too." Pa must have seen him, and they must have had a quarrel. David quickened his step, hoping the sooner to find out what had happened. A car passed him and stopped. It was Brother Dan.

"Thanks, Mr. Jenkins," he said as he settled into the seat beside the driver. "How are you today?"

"Well, young man, I'll tell you," Brother Dan said without a smile. "Ain't nothing wrong with me but the old age, and you better mind, 'cause it'll get you too some day."

They laughed together over the farm agent's favorite joke. David hoped the older man would not ask him any questions about going home at this time of day. There were other things to talk about. The return of Ed Williams. The prospect for crops this year. The heat and the need for rain. David was soon at his own gate.

His father had not come home. Ma was surprised and then disturbed to see David. When he had told her he had been fired, she fixed him some lunch and asked for details. You don't tell your mother everything. A man wants to protect those he loves from ugliness. David was trying to have his mother feel that he was discharged just because Mr. Boyd had gotten angry about something, something which had nothing to do with them.

"What time was this?" she asked.

"Oh, how do I know, Ma?" David laughed. "I'm not a clock watcher."

"David, did you see your father?"

"Why, no . . . No, Ma. Was he in town?"

"Did Mr. Boyd say anything about your father?" Ma asked.

David stuffed his mouth with cake and took a sip of milk.

"Believe he did mention him," he said. "Didn't say whether he had seen Pa or not. Maybe that's it, Ma. Maybe he don't want two Williamses on the payroll. We might get rich." He thought that wasn't bad.

Ma went to the window and pushed aside the curtain. She could see half a mile down the road toward South Town.

"I hope he comes home soon," she said.

David finished his lunch. He sat facing the back door, and through the screen he could see clean white clothes and colored shirts and Betty Jane's bright dresses drying on the line.

Rising from the table, he went to his mother. He was a whole head taller than she was. He put a hand on her shoulder.

"Don't worry, Ma," he said gently. "You got two men in the house now. I'm going to help you. Look, I'm going to take off these overalls, and just think, you won't have any more of these nasty, greasy things to wash."

"What about your father's?" Ma looked up at her tall son. She smiled, though.

David went into his room to change. He might as well wash the grease out of these himself.

And what about Pa? David was sure that his father had been there and that he was not going to work. He wished he knew what had happened.

Betty Jane came in to lunch. She was surprised to find her big brother at home, but she was glad. They had seen little of each other during the summer. When she came on the back porch, he was bent over the washtub, rubbing his overalls on the washboard with strong homemade soap.

She teased him and called him Sister Dave-Ella. He called her a little monkey, and she stuck out her tongue.

When he saw the car coming up the road, David went into the yard. He had been watching for it. He wanted to talk with Pa before his mother saw him. Ma had been watching too. She was as anxious to hear the news as her son was, but she did not rush out. It was just as well, she thought. Her menfolk stood beside the car talking. Neither of them was smiling.

David told Pa everything. The words rushed out. His watching for his father to come into the shop, Mr. Boyd's agitation, his sneer at the idea of a black doctor, his threat.

"It's bad, Son," his father said. "It's bad stuff. Rotten! He wanted me to go in the shop for forty dollars a week. Said we'd all have to take cuts. Just talked like it was business at first. Then I asked if the other mechanics were getting the same thing. That's when he got mad and said the war had ruined the Negroes, only he didn't say it that way. I guess I got mad too. I told him I wasn't willing to sell my skills for a mess of pottage. I told him just that. He said I'd come crawling to him for a job, said he'd fix it so I couldn't work anywhere, anywhere in South Town, in the county, in the whole state. He said the businessmen were going to get together and put the colored people in their place. I asked him what any man's place was. Then he started cursing, right there in front of the girls. He told me to pick cotton, shine shoes, lick the spit out of cuspidors. I said I'd rather do that than work at a skilled trade for peanuts."

Pa stopped and shook his head.

"He talked about integration and desegregation and said the white folks in this state didn't give a damn for the Supreme Court, and the black folks were fools if they believed in it." He smiled, but there was no humor in his face. "He didn't order me off the place. Guess he was saving that one for my son. I got off easy."

Ma waited as long as she could. Then she called through the open window, saying that dinner was ready.

"Just one more thing, Pa." David held his father's arm. "I didn't tell Ma very much. Just said that Mr. Boyd got mad and fired me. Check?"

"Check!" Williams put his hand on David's shoulder as they walked toward the back steps. He had to reach upward to do it. It felt good to both of them.

Dinner was on the kitchen table. Pa laughed and talked as though nothing had happened. It wasn't the usual Monday dinner of Sunday leftovers hastily prepared at the end of washday. Ma had cold sliced ham and some cold chicken from Sunday's dinner, but there were hot corn muffins and corn on the cob and string beans and lettuce and radishes, all from the garden. They drank iced tea, and then she took from the oven a peach cobbler and served it with whipped cream.

They ate slowly. Pa talked about the men he had seen in town. He told the funny things they had said and laughed at his own jokes.

When David asked to be excused, he invited Betty Jane

to go with him to the barn. Pa would want to talk to Ma alone.

"I have to do the dishes," Betty Jane said. "There's plenty of time. You help me with the dishes, and then I'll go with you."

"I'll let you milk," David promised.

Mrs. Williams told her to go ahead. She would do the dishes.

Betty Jane was happy to get away from the dishwashing. As they went down the path, Betty Jane carrying the milk pail, brother and sister talked about what they might do before school started. At least one picnic, and another day would be a fishing trip. They would go visiting. They would go to Belleville to see Mrs. Moss and to Center City to see the Johnsons and the Center City Williamses. They would have to go to the movies one or two nights. If Pa didn't go to work right away, maybe they could take a real trip, maybe to the coast where they could see where he had worked building ships.

David left Betty Jane milking to go for Josephine's fresh water. When he entered the barn again, she called him.

"David, what's the matter with Pa?" she asked.

David emptied the two buckets he carried into the big wooden tub. He moved it back toward the wall so Josephine would not kick it over during the night. He took as long as he could. He was thinking.

"Dave, you heard me. What's the matter with you, too?"

"What do you mean?" he asked, looking down finally at his sister. He could get an argument out of this. "What do you mean, what's the matter with grown-up people?"

"Oh, you think you're so grown up." Betty Jane smiled up at her brother. "You know what I mean. You all been acting funny, and Pa, he's been . . . I don't know . . . he seems like he's so much older since he's been back."

"Sure! Is that what you mean?" David acted as if it were very simple. "Sure he's older. You're older, ain't you? What's the matter with getting older? You're older today than you were yesterday. Pa's older now than he was when he started to work in the city. For gosh sakes! Older! Come on. You got to leave some milk in the bag for Josephine's milk snakes."

Betty Jane made a show of fright. She jumped and turned and almost upset the pail. David was fun.

When David and Betty Jane came in, Ma was laughing and Pa was drying dishes.

They started planning what they might do together. Betty Jane cried out for trips and visits, all the fun they would have, all the people they would see.

"Well, all right, chillen," Pa said. "Times a-wasting. Your hair is short and your feets is long, I don't see what you waiting on! Let's go. Let's get started."

"Oh, not tonight, dear," Ma said. "Why, we hadn't planned anything."

Betty Jane danced her delight.

"Well, we don't need a blueprint to find our way up the road," Pa said. "Do we, Dave?"

There was hasty washing, changing to fresh starched

clothes, slicking down of hair, and the family was off, with David driving and Betty Jane beside him. Pa and Ma rode in the back and called themselves bride and groom.

They went to see the Mannings. Mrs. Manning was one of their favorite friends. Indeed, she was a favorite friend of everybody for miles around. She was a widow and the mother of grown sons and daughters. Her youngest daughter was in college. Two of her sons were up North, where they were married and had families. Her granddaughter, Elizabeth, lived with her. Her youngest son, Al, had been in service. He was at home now. David liked to hear him talk about the things he had seen. Freed from the responsibilities of her own children, Mrs. Manning had gone back to teaching. In the two-room school at Holly Crossing, she saw before her the sons and daughters of those she had taught a generation earlier. Men who had traveled these years to the far corners of the earth wrote to her, "Dear Mother Manning."

Mr. Jackson, the principal, back early for the school year, drove up and stopped for a visit. He was eager to hear from Mrs. Manning a report on what had been happening among the people. He wanted to know what folks were saying about school integration.

"They don't say much," Mrs. Manning told him. "They don't expect any changes soon, and they don't see anything they ought to do but wait."

A full moon rose while they sat on the porch. Joshua, one of the men who was helping with the tobacco, came to say good night. He said he just happened to be carrying his guitar.

With little urging he sat on the steps and sang "Careless Love" and "Nobody's Darling."

Ed Williams laid aside his troubles. He had worked away from home for nearly three years without a break except for short week ends. Mrs. Williams said he had earned a vacation and she wanted him to take it. They made their visits. They went fishing at the millpond, and took Ben Crawford. David and Ben had to show where David had gone over the dam and just where and how Ben had pulled Little Red out and where David had been located by the white boy. On Sunday they went to Centerville.

They had their fun that first week. The second week started out with more fun, but it was not the same. Pa seemed restless again. He was a working man, and idleness was like Sunday clothes. It wasn't natural. He wasn't free and easy.

Ma had only words of encouragement. She agreed that Ed was doing the right thing. Of course he should not sell his skills for a mess of pottage. She would rather grub a mess of pottage out of their own piece of land. It was about paid for, thank the Lord. They had some savings. They could wait a while.

"For all his big talk," she said, "Mr. Boyd needs you more than you need him, and right away, too. He'll be the one to crawl, if anybody crawls. I don't see what makes him try to be so mean."

"Don't nobody have to crawl," Pa said. "Why should a

freeborn man have to crawl to anybody for anything? He can come to me like a man and say he needs my skill and say what he'll pay. If he offers enough, I'll work for him. I'll work good and earn him money. If he don't, I'll know what to do."

But Boyd did not come and say he needed Ed Williams. He drove by the Williams house while Ed sat on the porch. He drove by looking straight ahead. David saw the dull look in his father's eyes.

11

On Wednesday Ed Williams drove alone to South Town. He came back early, but he looked tired. David wondered if he had seen Mr. Boyd. Out in the yard, beyond Ma's hearing, he asked his father.

"Nope," Pa said. "I didn't see him, but I saw some others. He's been around. He's been to Chevvie and the other shops. They got together on me."

On Thursday he drove off again, this time away from South Town. He took his box of tools and a pair of overalls, saying he might be gone all day.

It was nearly dark when he got back. The car was covered with dust, but his overalls were still clean. They were folded just as they had been laid in the car.

11: SOUTH TOWN

On Friday it rained. Williams drove out to the road and turned toward South Town, and David knew he meant to explore the towns beyond.

Ma said she had wanted to do some shopping. It was plain to see that she was worried. She wasn't worried about how they could get along. They would make it. She was worried about the hurt look in her husband's eyes. It rained hard. Cars went by on the highway with the mounting and then fading sound of rubber on wet asphalt. Mr. Boyd did not stop. Nobody called.

It was nearly dark when Pa came home. He had that tired look. He said little. He did not smile. He ate and answered questions shortly.

After David had gone to bed, he heard Pa talking in the kitchen with Ma. David wasn't trying to listen for the words, but at one place Pa raised his voice.

"I ain't crawling to nobody." That was what David heard.

Before Pa went away to work in the city, the Williams family had established a regular Saturday routine. Ma would ride to South Town with her husband first thing in the morning when he went to work. As she did her shopping, the packages and bundles would accumulate in the car parked behind the garage. By noon Ma would be through with her business, and Pa would bring her home during his lunch hour. Then in the evening, after Pa came home and had his dinner, all the family would go back to town for Saturday night.

Stores and shops and markets stayed open late. Saturday

was pay day for those who worked. It was market day for those who bought and sold. Bargains were advertised. Payments on accounts were made. Debts were increased in the dazzle of Saturday night's display.

David remembered Saturday nights first as he trudged along holding to his father's hand, moving through the forest of legs and skirts, and then on the edge of the forest looking into brightly lighted show windows with his tongue licking across the coldness of an ice-cream cone.

When he was older, David walked alone. Sometimes he would find a boy he knew and walk with him, promising to be back at the car in just a little while. Time went fast on Saturday nights, and he had been punished for holding up the family, making his father wait and walk about to call and look for him, worrying his mother, who was always afraid he would get into trouble.

With Pa away, Saturdays had been different. In the morning Ma would catch a ride to town. People whom they knew would be passing. Often she would make a deal with the same friend to bring her back at a certain time. If not, she would deposit her packages as she shopped in the car of someone else who lived out that way. When the car owner came back to his car and found packages which did not belong to him, he knew he was going to have a rider. Sometimes it was confusing, but everybody was nice to Mrs. Williams.

Ma did not like David to go to town on Saturday nights. She seemed altogether unreasonable on the subject. David could see nothing to be afraid of in the town.

"I'm not a baby, Ma," he would say patiently. "And I don't run around with fellows who get into trouble."

David knew there was a crowd of boys, his age and a little older, who might have trouble. He knew them. They were just the fellows around who had dropped out of school. Some lived in town, and others lived on nearby farms. David felt that the members of that crowd were trying, deliberately trying, to be tough. As individuals he liked some of them. As a crowd they were headed in another direction. Nobody said anything about it, but David knew and the fellows knew that there was a difference. They were not walking together.

Most of the fights in South Town took place on Saturday nights. Older people gathered around Brown's restaurant. Younger people liked Jo-Jo's place because there was a large floor and they could dance to the music of the juke box. Both places sold wine and beer, but people seldom got drunk. At the barbecue stand only soft drinks were sold, but bootleggers met their customers there and sold country-made liquor illegally.

People who got drunk, really drunk, would be locked up by Chief Peebles or his assistant if either of the officers saw them. If friends were around, they would take care of the drunk, get him into a quiet place or get him into a car to his home.

No one liked to see a man locked up in the jail.

It wasn't a big jail.

It wasn't like in the pictures.

It was just about the size of a brick two-car garage

and it was in an alley; that is, it opened into the unpaved alley back of the liquor store. The door was of heavy wood, and it had riveted iron straps on it, and over the windows were iron bars. That hardly made it look like a jail, because doors and windows of warehouses are often secured the same way. You wouldn't have known it was a jail, just to look at it.

You would have to smell it.

Everybody who smelled the jail would know. They might not know it was a jail, but they would know that the place was something bad, something to keep out of and away from, something that was evil and cursing and fouling.

It wasn't a big jail, but Chief Peebles boasted that it was big enough for all the bad folks who wanted to jump in it. It was big enough to have two cells so white and colored offenders could be kept separated.

David had passed the jail with other boys. He knew the smell. He knew men, and some boys, who had been locked up there. He knew them, but they were not his friends. They were the ones who seemed deliberately to be tough and rowdy. Most of them were ignorant and very poor. It was said that no graduate of Pocahontas County Training School had ever been in jail.

Saturday morning broke clear. It had rained in the night, and the air was sultry, but the sun was bright. During the morning David worked in the garden. He turned some soil where he planned to put in late vegetables. His father had taken Ma and Betty Jane to South Town to do some shopping. David did not want to go so early in the day. There would be more to see in the late afternoon and after dark.

Pa brought Mrs. Williams and Betty Jane home at noon, and after lunch he went right back, saying that he had to see some friends. David was not through in the garden, and he hadn't washed up. It would be easy to catch a ride if his father did not come back with the car in time.

David had taken his bath and he was partly dressed when someone knocked, and then he heard his mother talking at the front door. He had put on his white trousers, which were a little short but not too short for wearing in a crowd. He was lacing his saddle oxfords when Betty Jane came to the door.

"Ma says come, David," his sister said. "It's the sheriff."

"The sheriff?" No officer of the law had ever been to their house. "What's he want?"

"Come on. They're talking." Betty Jane was frightened.

David hurried from the room, drawing a shirt over his arms.

The sheriff and another white man were in the front bedroom. The bed was pulled out from the wall, and the sheriff's man was bent over with a flashlight. The sheriff had Pa's gun in his hand.

"Who's this?" the sheriff asked Ma.

"This is our son," Ma said. Her voice was strained and hollow. "His name is David."

"What's the matter, Ma?" David went and stood close by his mother's side.

"Just a check-up, boy," the sheriff said easily. "You got a gun?"

David's mouth went dry. He licked his lips.

"Where's your old man's pistol?" the sheriff demanded.

"He hasn't got a pistol," David said. It was the truth. Ed Williams had always said a decent man had no need for a pistol.

"Don't lie to me, boy," the sheriff said. "If you're lying and we find out, we're liable to have to take you along. That's perjury, you know."

David knew it was not perjury, but he said nothing.

Ma said it was true that her husband did not own a pistol. He used to hunt with the shotgun. The sheriff seemed to believe her.

"You got a gun?" he asked David. "Any kind of a gun?"

"Yes, sir," David replied. "I've got a rifle, a twenty-two."

"Bring it here."

David looked at his mother, and she nodded quickly. As he started for his room at the back of the house, the two men came close behind him.

"You all got anything else?" the sheriff asked.

"No, sir, only my father's shotgun and my rifle," David said. He was about to reach for the .22 caliber pump gun where it hung on the wall when the sheriff's assistant shoved him aside. He took the rifle in his hands and threw open the breech, pumping it a couple of times. It was not loaded.

"Where's your cart'iges, and where does your old man keep his shells?"

David went to a shelf and took down a box containing a dozen or more longs. Then he went back into the front bedroom and got a box of sixteen-gauge shells. The two men searched every room. They looked into closets and moved things in the pantry. They went on the back porch and pulled a box away from the wall. They turned up the mattresses, even in Betty Jane's small room. They pulled the radio away from the wall and looked into the cabinet. They lifted pictures so that anything hidden behind them might fall to the floor.

Mrs. Williams, David, and Betty Jane followed them, not saying anything.

At last they seemed to be satisfied.

"Is anything wrong, Sheriff?" Ma asked when they were ready to go. "Can't you tell us?"

"It's just a routine check-up," the sheriff said, lighting a cigaret and throwing the match on the floor. "If you folks are telling the truth, it's all right."

"I don't understand." Ma wanted to know more. "Our home has never been searched before."

"We ain't searched it, woman," the sheriff said. "We ain't searched your house. We just asked you some questions, and you turned these pieces over to us voluntary for safekeeping."

"But we didn't," David said quickly.

"Oh, yes, you all did, boy." This time the sheriff's man spoke. He was smiling. "I seen you. I'm a witness."

When they had gone, Ma sat down in a low rocker. Betty Jane went to her, and Ma put an arm around the little girl's shoulder and held her tight. David hooked the screen door and stood there until the car had driven out of the yard and turned toward South Town.

"Your father is in trouble," he heard his mother say.

David turned.

"Pa don't get into trouble, Ma," he protested. "He ain't ever been in trouble. Not ever."

"He's in trouble, Son," Ma said, her eyes fixed straight before her. Betty Jane was crying. "Hush, baby. We've got to think. We've got to do something."

"I'll go in town, Ma," David said. "I'll catch a ride. I'll get help."

"Yes. You'll need help." Ma got up and put a hand on David's arm. "I'll go, too. Somebody in town will know. We'll try to find Mr. Jenkins. We'll go."

Betty Jane was still crying. Ma was putting on her hat when a car came up from South Town and turned into the yard. It was Joe Brodnax from the Ford agency. He braked swiftly and jumped from the car.

"They got Ed. They locked him up for nothing, less than nothing," he said.

He told all that he knew. Williams had come to the agency. He had found Mr. Boyd in the superintendent's office. Joe had heard Mr. Boyd talking about Ed's crawling back to work. Old man Boyd had been mean, and Williams had talked back to him, told him he had a right to work and be paid the same as other men. Boyd had stormed. Mundy had joined in. Mundy had said Williams was full of foreign Communist propaganda. Williams had come out of the office, with Boyd shouting that people were sick and tired of agitators and they were going to teach the Negroes a lesson.

"I knew something was going to happen," Joe went on. "After Ed left, the man was calling people on the phone. Then one of the Skipwith boys come to the alley door and called me out. He said Ed Williams was arrested. That's when I left to bring you all the word."

"What can we do?" Ma asked. "We never had anything like this before. What is it about bail?"

Joe stood silently looking at the floor. Ma shook his arm.

"Tell me what to do, Mr. Brodnax," she said. "Lawyers get people out of jail. Can't we get a lawyer?"

Joe looked up and shook his head. "Mrs. Williams, I don't know what to say. You can get a lawyer, maybe, but if old man Boyd wants Ed to stay in jail over the week end, they ain't nobody hardly can get him out. I'll drive you anywhere you say. I ain't going back to work today. It's pay day, but that don't matter."

They packed themselves into Joe's old coupe. Betty Jane sat on her mother's lap. They were crowded, and the car was dirty. It was the kind of car that automobile mechanics often drive. It had a sweet-running motor, but little else that was good could be said about it.

In town, people were sympathetic. All the colored people had heard that Ed Williams had been arrested for talking back to his former boss. They said it was a shame. Some of them had seen the arrest made near Brown's restaurant. Mr. Brown said he would do anything he could.

People were sympathetic, but they were powerless.

One of the tough boys, just a little older than David, came up and took off his hat.

"Mrs. Williams," he said, "I done talked to Mr. Williams."

Ma grabbed him by the arm.

"You went to the jail?" she asked.

"Oh, yes'm. Jailhouse ain't nothing to me. I talked to him through the window."

"I'll go there now."

"No'm. You can't do that," the boy said. "You're a lady. Can't no lady go up in that alley. He specially said to tell you and David not to come up there. He say tell you to stay home. He say have Mr. Jenkins get him a lawyer. Get Lawyer Wilson. He the best one in this town."

"Is he all right?" Ma said, still holding the arm of the boy who looked to her like a messenger of hope. "Did they hurt him?"

"Yes'm, he all right." He smiled. "They don't hurt you up there, not most and generally. He say he hope the lawyer get him out, though. It sure ain't no place for a man like Mr. Williams to stay the night."

"Will you go back?" Ma took money from her purse and held it out. "Can you go back and tell my husband that you have seen me? Tell him I'll do exactly what he says."

"Sure, I'll go back." He drew away. "I'll go tell him."

Mrs. Williams took a step forward, still holding out the

paper money. "Here, take this for your trouble," she said. "And I thank you. You don't know how much I thank you."

"Ain't no trouble. I couldn't take nothing." His smile was full and warming. "Mr. Williams been a friend to me, and he's a fine man. I'm glad to help."

They learned that Dan Jenkins had not been in town. Lawyer Wilson's office was closed. He was not at home, but Mrs. Williams left a message.

"Tell him," she said, "that whatever it costs we will pay. Be sure to tell him that."

They discussed driving back in the Williams car. David had a spare key, but they decided Mr. Williams would need the car to come home in. Mr. Brown said he would keep an eye on it. It was getting late. Pa had said for them to stay at home. Joe volunteered to come back and keep after Lawyer Wilson. Mrs. Williams said she hated to take up all his time.

"I don't mind that," Joe said. "I sure don't. I'll do anything for a man in trouble, and Ed's my friend. If they's any other place you want to go, we go there 'fore we leave town."

"How about the old judge?" David asked. "I think he could help us. He knows what kind of man Pa is."

Old Judge Armstead was heartily loved by the people of Pocahontas County. He was a kind man, and all the colored people said with great respect that Judge Armstead was a "sure enough gentleman." He was perhaps the best educated person in the county. David had heard that Judge Armstead had said publicly that the law applied equally to white and black.

11: SOUTH

They went to Judge Armstead's house.

Joe stopped his shabby car on the road. David walked with his mother up the driveway and knocked on the side door. A colored woman they knew worked in the house; she came to the screen door. She did not say it, but she seemed to know what their trouble was. She would call Judge Armstead.

While Ma told her story, the judge stood inside looking out over her head. It had been a hot day, and he had taken off his shirt and his shoes. Through the screen David could see the white hairs on his chest above the line of his undershirt. Blue veins stood out on his forearms. The muscles of his biceps looked soft.

"You people don't understand," he said, still gazing out as though he were searching for something far away. "You people don't understand that it's a matter of law. The case has not come before me. Now I hear your side. How do I know what the complaining witness and others will say? I can assure you that whatever decision I render will be in keeping with the law and the evidence presented."

"But can't we do something now, Judge Armstead?" Ma was almost in tears. "We've never had anything like this before. I don't understand those things. What about bail?"

"You will need counsel," the judge said. "You can get a lawyer next week when your man comes up for his hearing."

"Next week?" Ma would have fallen if David had not held her arm. "Next week? Must he stay in that place until next week?"

"I am afraid so." At last the judge looked into the eyes of the woman before him. "I am afraid it will be impossible to find a lawyer to take the case at this time."

He turned away and walked off silently in his stockinged feet.

David had to put his arm around his mother's waist to steady her as they walked down the drive to the car.

"Good-by, you all!" David looked back over his shoulder. The woman who had received them said softly, "God bless you, and be careful!"

God bless you and be careful. The benediction and the counsel. A word to cheer and a word to caution. What did it mean? A green light and a yellow, or was it a green light and a red? Might it be a warning? Was there another danger? What would they do?

Joe drove down by the high school for white children and turned to pass Lawyer Wilson's house; but they could see the garage standing open and empty, so they did not stop.

12

It was nearly dark when they got home. David had to hurry with his evening's work. Betty Jane offered to help him, but he told her to stay in the house with Ma and to call him if anyone came.

Ma prepared dinner in silence. Even David had lost his appetite. The food had no taste, but they sat at the kitchen table, each one trying to encourage the others.

There was a step on the back porch.

"It's me, Al. Don't turn on the light." Al Manning came in and moved through the kitchen to stand in the door of David's room in the shadow.

"Come on in, Reverend," he said, "in here." Reverend Arrington was panting.

"Mr. Williams ain't come home yet?" Al asked. "I just thought I'd come and sit with you. Reverend Arrington was at the house, and he wanted to come too."

"That was right nice of you, Al," Mrs. Williams said with a smile, "and you too, Reverend Arrington. Won't you folks sit down and have a bite? We didn't have much."

Reverend Arrington said he had eaten his dinner.

"That's all right, Mrs. Williams," Al said. "We ate before we left home. Ma says tell you she's with you in spirit."

"Come on and sit down," said David. "We don't charge for seats."

"Not worth while to get in the light," Al said. "You through eating? Come on in; I want to talk to you."

David went into his room, and in the dark they talked.

"You don't have to bother your mother," Al said softly, "but you might as well know there may be trouble Some of the folks are watching out in town, and some more will be out here. Some of the white folks have been having meetings. They're talking about putting us in our place. You got any guns in the house?"

David told in low tones about the sheriff's visit.

"That figures!" Al said. "They took the guns so you all wouldn't be able to fight back. It shows how well they've organized. Well, we're getting organized too. Come on up front."

They slipped through the kitchen door and on into the front room. The preacher, fat though he was, moved lightly behind them.

"When Ma slowed down for us to get out of the car, I put a bundle down on the far side of the road," Al said, pointing out a spot near a bush. "You'll have to go out there and get it. Don't let anybody see you, but if they do see you, it won't be like them catching sight of me."

"What do you think they'll do, Al?" David asked.

"Maybe nothing. Maybe nothing at all," Al said. "We just got to be ready."

David went out and sat on the steps of the porch. He watched his chance and ran across the highway, picked up the package, and was back in his place before the road was lit up again by the lights of a passing state police car.

The bundle was heavy. In the padding of an old patchwork quilt there were long straight pieces and other shapes which were tapered. David knew before Al unwrapped them in the darkness of the front room that they were guns, two shotguns and a repeater rifle.

Reverend Arrington had gone back to hold Mrs. Williams' attention.

"The others will be along soon," Al said, as he fitted gun stocks and barrels.

David told of their efforts during the afternoon. He said that Judge Armstead had seemed more concerned than he wanted to show. David still believed that somehow the law, as represented by Judge Armstead, would protect them. There was something dreamlike about the whole situation.

The white car of the state troopers passed, moving slowly.

"That's the second time they've gone by," Al said.

"Maybe they won't come in. If they do . . ." He paused.

"If they come, Al, what are we to do?" David asked.

"The preacher" — in the darkness Al motioned with his head — "Reverend Arrington is to talk to them, try to keep them from coming in. That's the diplomatic line of defense. If he can't stop them . . . we'll see."

Another car coming from the direction of South Town slowed up and then accelerated, and the car moved on.

"That's Ben Crawford's car," David said.

"They didn't stop because that other car was coming," Al said. "They'll be back."

Other cars passed, going up and down the highway. David hoped the Crawford car would wait awhile.

They watched for it.

It was coming, coasting without much noise. It slowed without coming to a full stop. A car door slammed, and the motor roared as the Crawford car sped off toward the town. Two bulky forms moved across the highway and merged into the shadow of bushes around the steps. Al went to the door and spoke.

With just the least bumping of hard metal against wood, Israel Crawford and his son, Israel, Jr., came in.

They reported that things were quiet in town, awful quiet. The state liquor store had closed early without explanation. Mr. Brown was not selling wine at his restaurant. He had taken all he had off the shelves.

Around the barbecue stand and at Skipwith's pressing shop, people were coming and going. They were not just standing by the road, hanging around like most Saturday nights.

White folks? What are they doing? Kind of hard to say. Some of them said they hoped there wouldn't be any trouble. Some of them had good hearts. Others were just plain scared. The rebbish ones weren't saying anything.

The light was switched off in the kitchen. The little glow that had come through the door was gone. The folks were coming to the front room. Ma was in the doorway with the smaller shape of Betty Jane beside her. The preacher leaned against the mantel over the fireplace.

David told his mother that everything was all right. There was nothing for her to worry about.

"I know, Son," she said. Her voice was strong, although she was speaking low. "It's all right. For a while I was afraid. I just didn't know which way to turn without Ed. I'm all right now, and I want to thank you all who have come. Al, you're a good boy, a son any mother could be proud of. I don't know who the others are by name, but I know you are true friends. God bless you."

Al brought her low rocker, and they told her Mr. Crawford and his son were there. She must have made Reverend Arrington tell all he knew. She was prepared for anything.

"I'm keeping up the fire," Mrs. Williams said. "There's coffee on the stove and cold ham and biscuits and some cake on the table. We might as well eat."

"Can we play the radio, Ma?" Betty Jane asked.

David felt it wasn't just right somehow for them to be

sitting around with a radio playing while Pa was in jail, but Ma snapped it on and they got some music.

While they waited, saying little, cars went up and down the highway. Some of them slowed down. Then two cars passed, driving very slowly. They passed, and then they pulled off the pavement and stopped. Their lights were put out. Al and Mr. Crawford went into the front bedroom to look from that side. Men were talking at the car. They could not have been friends. They were the others. Guns were loaded. Reverend Arrington stood with his broad shape framed in the little light that came through the door. It looked as if the men got back into their cars and drove off. Al came back.

"We've got to watch both sides and the back," he whispered. Each man was sent to a window with a loaded gun. David was to watch the back through the window from his own room. Israel, Sr., and Al took opposite sides. That left only the front with Reverend Arrington standing in the door. The Reverend did not have a gun. He was afraid of guns. He wasn't afraid of white people, though, and he sure could talk.

In the front room the radio had been turned off.

There was no moon. Crickets and other insects of the dark seemed less noisy this night. It was as though they too waited for a blow out of the silences. It was a long wait.

Troubled thoughts went through David's mind. What was the danger? He had heard of mob violence, and he had read newspaper accounts of beatings and shootings by organized groups of white people. He had seen pictures of crosses burning and houses destroyed by fire and bombs. It had always seemed far away, something that happened where people were different from the people around South Town. Yet he knew that it could happen. There were some mean people. His father should not have been arrested. Joe had held little hope for Pa's release. Judge Armstead had said no lawyer would take the case just now. The woman who worked for him had said, "Be careful."

There was no movement in the garden, nothing unusual in the barnyard. A rooster crowed, and others echoed his call. It must be after midnight, and nothing had happened.

David's mouth was dry. He was thirsty. He wanted to talk to someone. He wanted to go outside. He wanted to see what was out there. He left his window for a minute to go into the kitchen.

Israel Crawford leaned in the door, his rifle hooked in his good left arm. David spoke to him. No, he hadn't seen anything. David wanted to ask Israel how he could shoot with only one hand, but Israel did not turn his head. He just stood motionless, quiet. David drank some water. It was warm, but it refreshed him a little. When he passed the door again, Israel said without moving, "We ready!"

A little later Al's voice reached him from the kitchen. There was the sound of the coffee pot being moved. David's eyes searched the darkness for movement. Al came and stood beside him.

"You'd better go drink some coffee," Al said. "I'll watch here."

David said he didn't like coffee, but he'd get some milk.

"No milk, Dave," Al said. "Milk will make you sleepy. Drink a cup of coffee and then go up front. Your mother will feel better if you're up there."

David drank the coffee. It was very strong. It took a lot of sugar to make it go down.

Ma had put Betty Jane to bed. Poor kid. This wasn't for little girls.

They told him more cars had come and stopped on the road. People sure were looking them over. The white state police car passed again.

David felt more comfortable here in the front. Ma was sitting in her rocker behind him, and out the side window where he watched, he could see the highway toward South Town. Among the cars that went by were those of friends. He could be sure about them. He knew the noises they made as well as their shapes and the way their lights were canted or dim on one side.

A car stopped in front of the house. A man got out and stood. He came slowly toward the yard and stopped at the gate.

It looked like a white man. David stood in the door beside the preacher. He cocked his gun. He heard the click of another safety behind him.

"Hey, there." The voice was familiar. "This is McGavock. Anybody home?"

"Mr. Mack?" David called.

"Davie, can I come in?" McGavock moved forward

slowly. He was opening the gate. He carried a gun.

"Stop where you are!" It was Al speaking over David's shoulder.

"He's all right," David said. "He's our friend. He's a mechanic who worked with Pa at the garage."

"Put your gun down and come in," Al said. "Can you trust him?" he asked David.

"He's all right, I tell you," David insisted.

McGavock laid his gun on the grass and came up on the porch.

"We heard about it, and we thought we'd come out and set up with you," he said, speaking through the screen door. "It's Travis in the car, Dave. You know Travis."

"Sure, Mr. Mack." David had not seen Travis since the white mechanic was discharged from the shop. "Sure, tell him to come on in. Some others are here already!"

"I don't know about that," Al said, pushing by David to go out to the porch.

"Young man, you don't need to be afraid of us," McGavock said. "I don't blame you for not trusting me, but I swear I'm with you. So's Travis. He brought me the news. Soon or late you might need us, and we're ready."

It took Ma and David to convince Al that there was no trickery in the offer, that these men had proved before that they were friends. It was Al who finally went out to the highway to tell Travis to put the car in the empty garage and come in.

Things were still quiet in South Town, McGavock reported, but after Boyd had Williams arrested on charges of disturbing the peace, he had gotten some of his friends together. They were talking about teaching the colored folks a lesson, putting them back in their place, they said. It was the old night-rider plan, to terrorize the family and, through them, all the colored people of the countryside. The sheriff and the police were with Boyd, of course, and those who were right thinking were afraid to do anything.

McGavock did not know the part Reverend Arrington was to play, and when he saw the white car passing again, he suggested a plan.

"Why don't you let me set out there on the porch?" he asked. "They know me, and if they come, I got a nice speech prepared for 'em. They know me, and they know I mean what I say." He turned toward Al. "Maybe you don't trust me, but one thing you all got to remember, it ain't every white man that's against colored folks. A lot of us feel just like you do. It's just that we been scared too, and we keep silent about what we think. I'm through biting my tongue now. I want a chance to say my speaking piece."

Al was still doubtful, but he said, "We'll try it."

He was grim, and he spoke between scarcely parted lips. "We'll be watching you, though, you and your friend. If it gets bad, I'll know what to do."

McGavock turned and pulled himself up tall.

"I'm an old man, son," he said, "and I wouldn't mind dying for something good. I'd be scared only of dying as a traitor. You can trust me."

Al watched while McGavock went to get his gun and returned to sit on the edge of the porch, partly hidden by the climbing gourd vine. Inside, no one spoke until Al opened the door and started telling the men to get back to their posts.

"We got plenty in the house now," Israel, Jr., said. "Maybe I better get out front. I'll be up yonder, 'longside the fence."

Travis spoke. "Good idea!" he said. "Flank defense. How's about me going with you?"

Al looked at Travis. In the darkness there was little he could see.

"No! Israel won't need help," he said. "You'll be with me."

The house settled into quiet again.

Men left their places one at a time to go to the kitchen for coffee. Ma went back to put more wood on the fire. Those who smoked covered the glow of their cigarettes so that they would not be seen by those who drove by.

The world lay quiet outside. Few cars passed. Although he drank more coffee, David was sleepy. A sentry does not sleep at his post. At their places men still crouched, peering into the darkness. Mrs. Williams sat back in her rocker with her eyes closed. She was not asleep, or if she was, she slept fitfully, because the chair moved and she sighed. They were not afraid. They knew fear, but they were not afraid of whatever was to come.

The little creatures of the night quieted. It must be near morning. It was a long night.

The silences. These were the silences, then. About him were people who were no longer satisfied with silence. The preacher was here, ready to do what he could. Al Manning had brought the courage of a trained soldier. Mr. Crawford, who had lived in and with the silences all his life, had come with his battle-scarred son, and they were ready to speak out. Travis and Mr. Mack had come, not afraid and not willing to keep silent.

A schoolhouse on a hill should ring out in the silences. The fresh paint had made the school look like a lighthouse. It called the people to learn. It gave them something to stand up for. It made them know what to speak for, and it gave them courage. Israel Crawford had said, "We're ready!" Judge Armstead had said there was nothing he could do. Maybe he was afraid.

Pa had spoken out, all right.

"I ain't crawling to nobody," he had said. He had talked back to a white man, and for talking back, Pa was locked up in the jail. David wondered if Boyd's hatred might lead him directly to the jail. He remembered things he had read about colored men dragged from their cells. No. Not that, he told himself, not just for back talk.

David's head rested against the side of the window as he studied the sky for a trace of light. The darkest hour is just before the dawn. This must be it, the darkest hour, but he, David Williams, was seeing things now he had never seen before. His eyes were being opened. There were good men and bad men. Travis and McGavock were white, but they had come to be with the colored, to speak out, to fight back, willing even to die with them.

That one word, *with.* Fighting with could mean fighting against, or could it? Should it? You had a fight with somebody, or you stood with somebody to fight an enemy. Words were funny. Words were like people. They were all about you, and you thought you knew them, and then they came up meaning the opposite of what you had thought they meant. And when you used them wrong and accepted them wrong, you were so sure you knew. You had been sure you were right until you learned better.

Eyes, but they see not. Ears, but they hear not. A blind man seeing and a man looking into darkness and seeing. A boy looking into the darkness and seeing the light, waiting in the silences and hearing a great voice ring out.

Cars were coming up the highway from South Town, moving slowly. David called out to the others. He counted six cars coming on close together. The white car of the state troopers was leading; as it came near, a spotlight was snapped on. The narrow beam played on the front of the house. There was a rush of feet from the rooms at the back. The head car stopped in front of the gate, its light shining through the door and flooding the room. Al and Travis and old man Crawford crouched silently, gripping their guns. The shadow of McGavock's form was thrown backward, jagged against the mantel over the fireplace.

"What do you want?" McGavock's voice rang out.

From the car a man replied, "What are you doing there?"

McGavock shouted, his voice echoing through the house, "I'm Sam McGavock. I'm a freeborn citizen, and I'm setting up with my friends. I'm asking you, what in God's name do you aim to do?"

There was no answer. Behind the police car, the others had stopped. In the house they could hear the drift of voices.

From the car someone called, "You're a white man, Mack. You got no business mixing up in this. If you know what's good for you, you'll clear out."

McGavock answered, "Yes, I'm a white man, and I ain't yellow, and I know what's good for me and what's good for you, too. If any one of you tries to harm anyone in this house, it'll be the last evil thing you do on God's green earth. We'll shoot, and we'll shoot to kill. And I know you, John Whitlock, parading in a uniform of the law, disgracing the mammy that born you. I know you, and I hate your guts. I hate what you're a-doing. Leave these people be."

McGavock turned toward the other cars. "And that goes for the rest of you," he shouted. "There ain't going to be no house-burning here tonight. Clear out now! Clear out! Get on back to your homes and your women whilst you're able, and come sun-up, look on the day and thank God you're living and beg Him to forgive you. This here's Sam McGavock talking sense to you, and by God you know I mean it."

The spotlight was turned off. A car door slammed, and two men walked forward to the police. Angry voices rasped through the night, and from the darkened cars ugly words were hurled at McGavock.

Another voice shouted out from somewhere in the darkness up alongside the fence. The voice was strong, but the tongue-twisting curses were not clear. Israel Crawford, Jr., had not yet mastered his false teeth.

"We ready for you . . . Oh, yes, we ready . . . Ain't nobody scared . . . Can't die but once, and if I dies, you dies with me . . . Come and get it, or get from round it . . . Maybe we goes down, but we goes down fighting and them what lives is living like mens . . . Get going now, white folks . . . Get in or get out . . . I tired of waiting . . ."

A starting motor whirred. The last car in line backed and turned and started back down the grade toward South Town. Another car pulled out. It did not turn, but headed up the hill away from town, rushing at full throttle as it passed the point closest to the hidden voice. The lights of another car lit up the highway briefly, and David recognized the heavy figure of Boyd as he left the police car and returned to his own.

They were leaving. The police car which had led the line was the last to leave — and it moved slowly with its spotlight playing along the side of the road.

Israel's voice shouted out again.

"If you come back, we still ready . . . Any time you want put this kind of mess on our folks, we be ready . . . Ain't going stand for no more lynchings . . . We fighting back . . . We ready."

The white car slowed and almost stopped, as though the driver would come back to meet the challenge. Then suddenly it leaped forward with a roar to overtake the other cars.

It was over. It was over for the time at least. David filled his lungs again and again. It was as though he had been under water for a long time, and now at the surface he could breathe.

McGavock sat on the step. His head was bowed into his hands. In her rocker Ma was weeping softly. David rested his gun in a corner and went to put his arms around his mother. He knelt by her chair and drew her head to his shoulder. He was like a man comforting his child.

"Ed, Ed!" she sobbed. "God help him! Don't let them get him."

"No, Ma. They wouldn't try that." David remembered that Joe Brodnax and the others were on guard in town. They too were ready.

"The Lord is my light and my salvation; whom shall I fear? The Lord is the strength of my life; of whom shall I be afraid?"

It was the preacher, quoting scripture at a time like this! David wanted to rise up and tell him to save it.

"When the wicked, even mine enemies and my foes, came upon me to eat up my flesh, they stumbled and fell. Though an host should encamp against me, in this will I be confident. One thing have I desired of the Lord, that will I seek after; that I may dwell in the house of the Lord all the days of my life, to behold the beauty of the Lord, and to enquire in his temple."

Maybe it was all right. Ma was quieter. She seemed to be listening. She seemed to get something out of it.

"For in the time of trouble he shall hide me in his pavilion; in the secret of his tabernacle shall he hide me."

Ma was joining in, her soft voice blended with that of the preacher. She knew every word of the psalm.

"And now shall mine head be lifted up above mine enemies round about me; therefore will I offer in his tabernacle sacrifices of joy; I will sing, yea, I will sing praises unto the Lord."

Mr. Mack opened the screen door and came in, leaning on one side, listening. Israel, Jr., stood outside the door, quiet again. No one else was speaking, just the preacher and Ma reciting from the Bible.

"Hide not thy face far from me; put not thy servant away in anger; thou hast been my help; leave me not, neither forsake me, O God of my salvation."

Another voice had joined in, faltering at first, then stronger. David raised his head and saw Al holding his gun at the ready and speaking the words his mother had taught him before men took him from home and taught him to kill.

"Deliver me not over unto the will of mine enemies; for false witnesses are risen up against me, and such as breathe out cruelty. I had fainted, unless I had believed to see the goodness of the Lord in the land of the living."

Then David joined in, and Mr. Crawford, and Mr. Mack, and Travis and Israel at the door.

"Wait on the Lord; be of good courage, and he shall

strengthen thine heart; wait, I say, on the Lord."

When he came to the end of the psalm, Reverend Arrington said, "Let us pray."

The words the preacher said were not in the loud speech of the church house on a Sunday morning. It was not as though he were calling to his God high in the heavens. It was rather as though he spoke to One who was there in the living room of the small white house at the side of the road a few miles from South Town. And the words asked for nothing. They expressed simple thanks for protection and deliverance from evil. David was kneeling beside his mother's chair. He was thinking that she seemed to be at ease when suddenly someone in the room shouted in alarm, and in the same instant came a roar that was a clatter and a series of sharp explosions and crashings and startled cries and rushing to get to guns laid down too soon. And then David saw through the window that cars were speeding down the road toward South Town, and in the next instant Israel stood on the porch firing after them and old Mr. Mack was there beside him, but the cars were out of range. Inside the house Al was calling for a light and Betty Jane was screaming in fright or perhaps in pain. David had to know, and he went to his mother, who was trying to comfort the little girl, and from her voice rather than the words she was saying, David knew that Betty Jane was not hurt and that Ma too was safe.

Betty Jane was not hurt, and Ma was safe, but Al was muttering strong curses as he bent to examine, with the light of a match, the face of Travis. Someone turned on the electric light. It was blinding at first, but they could see the mark of a bullet wound almost in the center of the forehead of the still white face.

David tried to remember what the limping veteran had once said about being with angels.

13

There was no panic in the house.

There was no panic, and for a time there was no movement. It was as though all thought and speech and motion were frozen in time and space.

Al was bending over the body of Travis where it lay, arms widespread, quite calm, the face upturned with the small red spot near the center of the forehead. The eyes were nearly closed. The mouth was slack. A slow stream of blood coursed from the hole and ran down to the side toward the right ear.

It was Crawford, father of Israel, who had reached up to pull the cord, flooding the room with light. He had not lowered his arm. His hand still clutched the small white ball on the end of the cord. Words came from him, in anguish. "Lord have mercy!"

Betty Jane, sobbing now, with her head on her mother's bosom, had not yet seen. Mrs. Williams was trying to hold the child's face away. Her eyes were wide as she rocked slowly, murmuring comfort to Betty Jane, and trying to understand that this was real and not a fantastic dream from which she would soon awaken.

Israel, standing in the door, clutched his gun with his one hand. The barrel was hot. His shooting had been too late. His one-armed aiming, he knew, had been far off target. He cursed himself for having left his post down by the road, where he would have seen the cars coming back for their sneak attack.

Reverend Arrington's first thought was that the prayers had been offered too soon. Then he remembered, and he spoke softly, "Greater love hath no man than this . . . that a man lay down his life for his friends."

McGavock was the first to move. He took off his jacket and, going to his friend, knelt and carefully lifted the head and put the folded jacket under it. Then he smoothed the dead man's hair and straightened his body and lifted the hands to fold across the breast. When McGavock had done all these things, the others were moving. Mrs. Williams had taken Betty Jane out, still keeping the little girl's face turned away. She returned with a sheet and one of her best white towels. This she laid folded over Travis's face. With McGavock's help, she spread the white sheet. The crease of the sheet went straight down the middle from the even roundness of the head where the Turkish towel softened the lines of the face to the little valley between the feet.

Daylight was coming on. The house was filling up with those who had heard the fusillade of gunfire. It was bad. It was not over. It would call for a different kind of fight now. Reverend Arrington insisted that only those who had been in the house at the time of the shooting should remain. The sheriff would have to be notified. He suggested that Mr. Mack go in to town for the officer. McGavock said he was willing, willing to do anything, but he would rather stay in the house. He wanted to wait with the others to do whatever he could do when "the law" came.

It was good that McGavock was present when finally the sheriff arrived. Al Manning had driven over to his mother's house to telephone a report to the sheriff's office at the county seat. Mrs. Manning had come back with him to be with Mrs. Williams. The men who came in cars and on foot would not leave in spite of the preacher's words. Most of them carried their guns openly. Many of them were heard to say that they wished they had been there in the night.

The sun was high. To David, who had not slept at all, it seemed especially bright on the whitewashed fence posts, and on the state troopers' white car which came second in the line of cars which the sheriff led up the highway from South Town. It was broad day, and there could be neither sneak attack nor ambush, but the armed men who came representing the law and those who waited in the house and on the porch and those who stood on the ground and sat in their own cars, all of them were alert for whatever might happen.

"We cannot fight the law," the preacher had said. "We will probably have to go to jail. That will be the time for those on the outside to help." He had written the names and addresses of people whom Mrs. Manning was to notify by long distance telephone.

"You'll find you have friends right here in South Town," McGavock had added. "I'll be with you in everything, and I know they won't keep any of us locked up; though, like you say, the sheriff will have to take us in."

The cars stopped on the road without moving from the pavement. The sheriff and three others got out of the first car. There was brief conversation with two state troopers and others. The sheriff and one trooper and four others, all carrying guns, came into the yard and, looking neither to right nor left, walked up the path and into the house. David held open the door. The trooper walked straight through the room to check the back of the house. The sheriff spoke sharply to McGavock.

"What happened?"

McGavock spoke slowly, deliberately choosing his words, fully aware that the sheriff knew half the story already.

"When they fired that volley from the road, they killed young Travis. They murdered him, and I know some of them who were in the crowd. I'm ready to give sworn testimony."

"Never mind that now." The sheriff turned away. "Who is the dead nigger?"

No one spoke as he bent to lift the sheet.

"Why, he . . . he . . ." The others moved forward to share his surprise.

"Yes," McGavock said, "yes, he's a white boy. He's the young vet with a wooden leg. A friend of mine, and somebody's going to pay for this murder."

"You're mighty damn right." The sheriff was shouting the words. "You're all under arrest. Every nigger on the place, and you too, McGavock. Whitlock!" — speaking to the trooper — "get them rounded up. Get them all rounded up. Get their guns and shoot down anybody that gives you trouble. I mean blow their brains out if they start any mess!"

Thirty-one Negroes and one white man were arrested that third Sunday in August in Pocahontas County. The event was widely reported in the press. There were pictures, pictures of the house, the stack of weapons which were seized. There were pictures of the county jailhouse, three stories high, modern, and of the courthouse with its four great white columns, and of the monument inscribed to "Our Gallant Confederate Dead" which decorated the center of the square in front of the courthouse. The monument was a favorite resting place for tired colored farm hands. They sat and lounged and told their stories there, and sometimes laughed and did shuffle-foot dances in the center of the square. They loved to pose for the pictures.

It looked as if it would be a big case. The hotels and

boarding houses were filled before Sunday passed, and all night more people were arriving. Hotels and boarding houses were filled with white guests, and it appeared that an equal number of "foreign" Negroes came. They too asked questions, and they took pictures. They rushed about in cars with upstate license plates, and they did not seem afraid of anything. Colored lawyers, never before seen in the county, arrived on Monday, and they went into the courthouse and demanded answers from the clerks, and the clerks could not give answers. It was said that the lawyers represented the National Association for the Advancement of Colored People.

On Tuesday morning the head jailer, without explanation, released the thirty-one Negroes, including Mrs. Williams and Mrs. Manning and little Betty Jane. McGavock had been released on Sunday afternoon. Four colored lawyers met them in the corridor and told them that they were free to go, with no charges against them.

Mrs. Williams, clinging to the arm of her son as though she would never again let him go from her side, asked the lawyer nearest her about her husband.

"Perhaps you know about him," she said. "Ed Williams. He was locked up in the South Town jail."

The lawyer was a tall man, light brown with curly hair. His smile was warm and hearty.

"Why, yes, Mrs. Williams," he said. "Mr. Williams should be released this morning. Right about now."

"Is he all right?" she asked. Her fingers dug into David's

arm. He did not mind. He knew how worried his mother was. "Is he all right?"

The lawyer looked surprised. He started to answer; then he said, "Why, I don't really know. I guess he's all right." He looked about and said to Mrs. Williams, "Excuse me." Then he turned hastily and shouldered his way through the crowd and out the door as the others moved out and down the steps.

Ed Williams was not all right.

When they finally got home, to the bullet-marked white house, they found that Ed Williams was not all right.

Dan Jenkins, the county farm agent, drove the Williams family home from the big brick building at the county seat. He explained that he had been in the other end of the county and news of the trouble had not reached him until Sunday. Then he had rushed back to South Town, and he had got busy seeing people of influence. He went to see old Judge Armstead. He even went to see Mr. Boyd. Mrs. Williams, riding beside him, said nothing. She sat leaning forward, as though by her will to reach her husband she could help the car. David, riding in the back seat with Betty Jane, was looking at Brother Dan as though he had not seen the older man before.

Jenkins talked a great deal, and he talked fast, like one who tries to explain away his failure. He had gotten in touch with the families of those who had been arrested. He had helped some of the womenfolk to get the cars which had been left at the Williams place. He did not ask how it felt for a woman like Mrs. Williams and a girl like Betty Jane to be in jail. He did not ask David how he had spent his time. Mrs. Williams asked about her husband, but Brother Dan had no word. No, he had not gone to the South Town jail.

He had been to see the family of the Travis boy.

"It was too bad about that young man," he said, "but of course he shouldn't have been there that night in the first place."

"No, Brother Dan," Mrs. Williams said quickly, "you should not say that. That young man, and Mr. McGavock with him, came to us as friends, to help us, to protect us."

"Just the same, he wouldn't be dead today if he hadn't been there. You have to admit that."

"It was a sacrifice," Mrs. Williams said, "a cruel, unnecessary sacrifice. It could have been one of us."

"You don't understand these things." Brother Dan turned to look at Mrs. Williams, and he looked back at David. "You see, that Travis boy was a Communist. Mr. Boyd himself told me."

"No, no! He wasn't. I knew him well." David was shouting his protest. "I know why Mr. Boyd would say that." He went on to tell of the incident when Travis had been fired and of the words Travis had said. He told about the night when he and Travis had walked the dark road from up by the Crawford place, and he remembered what Travis had said about catching the bus and riding in the Jim Crow seats at the back "with the angels."

Jenkins did not argue. He only shook his head from side to side as David talked, and then he said, "You don't understand these things. You are young. You don't understand."

Several cars were in the yard when Brother Dan made his left turn from the highway at the Williams house.

As Jenkins braked to a stop in the driveway, David recognized the car ahead.

"Dr. Anderson's here!"

Mrs. Williams was out of the car and running for the back steps when Mrs. Crawford appeared in the door.

"Not worth while to upset yourself," she called, as she walked down the steps to meet Mrs. Williams. "He'll be all right." She took Mrs. Williams in her arms, holding her back from rushing into the house. "He be worried about you, though. We didn't tell him where you all were. He not hurt bad, only you mustn't take on and get him excited."

David went ahead as Mrs. Crawford led his mother, calming her, up the steps and across the back porch, into the bright, sweet-smelling kitchen, and through toward the front bedroom. The clean smell of lysol and medicines was mixed with an unpleasant stench of body odor and filth. David saw his father in bed. He lay on his back, eyes closed. His face was bruised. Dr. Anderson was just closing his bag. He looked up, smiling, as Mrs. Williams went by David to reach her husband. At the sound of a little cry that Mrs. Williams could not hold back, her husband opened his eyes. He smiled and reached to take her hand.

"Hi, Pet," he said softly. "You all right? Doc says I'll be all right directly."

The doctor said he should not talk. Something in the medicine would help him to sleep. He would need sleep. He had been hurt, but there were no serious injuries. He said that he had brought Mr. Williams home, and he gave instructions for care, promising to come back late in the evening.

"What about you?" he asked Mrs. Williams. "Is there anything? Or the child?"

Mrs. Williams replied. There was nothing. No, they had not been hurt, not physically. She could not speak of the humiliation and the anguish of the hours.

"I feel dirty," she said. "I feel that I'll never be clean again."

She told David to gather up his father's clothes. They would be burned. All of their clothes that had been worn were foul. They would pour kerosene on them and burn them — everything, the shoes too.

Ed Williams did not talk. He did not seem to follow the conversation. His eyes were open, though. He seemed to be in a daze. He kept looking around the room and raised his head from the pillow to turn and look as though he were not really sure of something. He looked at the framed pictures on the wall and at the smaller pictures on the mantel and at Ma's little porcelain dogs sitting in a row. He looked at the things on the dresser, the can of talcum, the fancy bottles of perfumes and toilet waters, at the Christmas-stickered bottle of shaving lotion which Betty Jane had given him, and at the snapshots tucked in at the edge of the mirror. Then he looked back at his wife, and he answered to her smile. He made a motion as if to get up, but when she went to him, he lay back, and she talked to him and held his hand. Then he knew that he was at home with the things and the people he loved. His eyes closed, and he slept.

After bathing and dressing in clean clothes, David was in the back yard about to put a match to the pile of kerosene-soaked clothes when he remembered to go through the pockets of his father's clothes. They were empty.

Betty Jane came out to stand beside him and watch as he stirred the smoking fire with a stick.

"What you reckon they did to Pa?" she asked.

"I don't know." David was wondering the same thing. "They hurt him. He's got a cut on the left side of his head. I guess they beat him. I hate white folks."

"Mr. Travis was a white man," Betty Jane reminded him. "And there's Mr. Mack, and Dr. Anderson."

David remembered. While the fire burned, smoky with oil and rags, David remembered. Travis had said that changes were going to be made. McGavock had said that not every white man was against colored people. With his stick David reached into the burning pile and dragged out one of Pa's shoes. It had not burned at all. He wondered what might have happened if they had not been prepared when the mob came. Would the house have been burned? Would some one of the family have been killed? Suppose Pa was hurt worse than the doctor thought he was. David dropped the shoe on top of the pile. In time it would be consumed, in this fire or in some other; he would see to it that all of it would be burned.

As David looked away from the fire, he saw Harold Boyd and Little Red coming up the drive. Somewhere back in his mind David noted that Harold was not driving his convertible. What was he doing here, anyway, David thought. He hated Harold and all the Boyds.

"Hello, David," Harold said.

David didn't answer him.

"Hello, Betty Jane." Harold spoke again.

Still no one answered him. David noticed that both boys were tanned from their summer at the beach. Harold's hair looked blonder than ever against the brown of his skin. As David looked at them, his body grew tense with his hatred. They were the white folks who had hurt his father. They belonged to the man who had caused all the misery the Williams family had been through, the awful ache in their hearts. David hated them.

Betty Jane took a step nearer her brother. Neither of them spoke.

A deep flush crept up under Harold's tan. He dropped his head. "We've been away," he said, without looking up.

"Why didn't you stay away?" David said bitterly. "Why don't you and your kind stay away from here forever? Coming around scaring kids, hurting decent people, killing them. What did you come for? Do you want to see my father, see if they gave him a bad enough beating? Get out of here! I hate you — and everyone like you!"

Harold did not raise his head, but his right hand came up. He held his arm outstretched as if to ward off the sting of David's words.

"Don't say that, David," Harold said. "What I came for is to say I'm sorry for what happened. I want to do something to make up for it, if I can."

"What can you do?" David jeered. "Get in your fancy car and scare colored people off the road — "

"Don't," Harold pleaded. "I'm ashamed of that; I'll never do anything like that again — never. Not to you or anyone.

"David," Harold went on, head up now, meeting David's eyes, "I don't speak for my folks, but lots of people are sick about what went on here. They want to see to it that nothing like that happens again, and that's the way I feel. I'm thinking different, and I'm going to act different and do everything I can to make things better.

"I guess there isn't any more to say. We'd better go." Harold turned away, then looked back. "Will you tell your father and mother we came to say we're sorry?"

"Yes, Dave," Little Red added, "tell them we're sorry for everything." It was the first time the younger boy had spoken.

"I'll tell them," David said.

"Good-by, David," Harold called.

"Good-by," David answered. He added, "Thanks for coming."

He thought as he saw Harold and Red walking up the road that they were walking because it didn't seem right to come here in Harold's fancy car.

As David and Betty went inside, the shoe on top of the flaming pile was beginning to burn.

14

For some time there was no laughter in the Williams house.

There was no loud talking that day, or noise of any kind. Friends came to bring flowers. From their homes they brought fragrant roses and giant dahlias and early chrysanthemums. Bachelor's button and tall spikes of larkspur stood in jars by the fireplace in the front room. The women brought their offerings of flowers and food and services. They put their arms around Mrs. Williams and said their God bless you's and then left quietly.

Under the calming influence of the medicine, Ed Williams slept until late afternoon, when his wife awakened him and had him eat something. He sat up and he ate and he took more medicine. He answered their questions, but when he spoke, his voice was thick. When they said he should lie down again and go to sleep, he obeyed as a sick child would. Later the doctor came and examined him again. Dr. Anderson asked about David, and Mrs. Williams called her son from the porch where he was talking with Al Manning.

Dr. Anderson, sitting in Mrs. Williams' low rocking chair beside the bed, looked up and spoke to David.

"Your father had some bruises, but there is nothing too serious, physically anyway. He will be all right in a few days. But about you, David, and your mother —" He paused as he looked from David to his mother and back again to David. "I am really concerned about you. I don't know how much all this means to you. I'm hoping it won't hurt you too much, bad as it has been."

"I appreciate your interest," Mrs. Williams said softly. "I guess I'm worried about the same thing. How much more do we have to stand? Where will it end?"

"Well, I can tell you this: There won't be any more of it." Dr. Anderson spoke with a confidence that made David and his mother almost believe him. "The decent people of this county will see to that. A committee of the leading citizens has already been to see the sheriff and Chief Peebles. If you want to stay here, you will not be in danger. I'll guarantee it."

"How could we know?" asked Mrs. Williams. "How could we ever feel safe? Why have they done these things?

Who was it that beat my husband? What will they do next?"

Dr. Anderson took out his pencil and started marking a design on his prescription pad.

"I guess there are no simple answers to your questions," he said slowly. "Prejudice is not a matter of logic or reason, and it is not easy to explain the fear and hatred and the evil acts of prejudice. I don't know the names of those who did the beating. Do you really want to know?"

David was not surprised to hear his mother answer, "No."

"Of course people don't admit they are prejudiced," the doctor went on, "but they talk about white supremacy and sacred traditions, and they go to great lengths to keep Negroes in an inferior place. They don't think they are being mean. They claim to be trying to teach colored people to behave. They become very self-righteous about it, as though they had a duty to perform. So they scold, they threaten, and when words fail, they use force. If they could control Ed Williams and his family, they think all the other colored people would be frightened into staying in their places."

As he paused, David spoke up, asking a question long in his mind.

"Dr. Anderson," he said, "could you tell us what they mean by our place? What do they want us to do?"

Dr. Anderson smiled as he tried to answer.

"That's a good question, but see this, David. You recognize yourself as a boy, and you don't try to set your strength or your ideas against those of your father, who is a man, do you?" David agreed, and Dr. Anderson went on. "So your father has a place which is really above yours, and your father might be annoyed if you wanted to act as a man. Now, haven't you heard white people speak of colored men as boys and of colored women as girls? This is the place for colored people. They should occupy in society the place of children, not voting, not knowing too much or owning too much. They should be obedient and satisfied, and they should above all be respectful toward white people."

"How long do they think people should be children?" Mrs. Williams asked.

"As I said, there is no reason or logic to race prejudice. Progress is being made all the time. Not all white people, even in the South, think this way. In spite of what happened last week, things are better now than they were; and in some places, I understand, you might be very comfortable, and the children could grow up to forget this."

Dr. Anderson turned to David.

"You told me you wanted to be a physician. Do you still feel the same way?" he asked.

"Yes, sir, I do."

"Where would you want to set up practice?" he asked. Then he hurried on. "In the North some place, I guess. After all, this is a pretty bad place for colored people."

"I hadn't ever thought about going away, Doctor," David said, "except for schooling, of course. The people here need doctors. They need more than doctors; they need all kinds of people with training and skill and education. I hadn't thought of leaving to stay."

"That's very true." The doctor seemed pleased. "It's true that this section does need doctors and more education among all the people. I am sure you could help them in many ways."

The doctor paused and drummed his long sensitive fingers on the arm of the rocker. David looked at them and saw that though he was beating time, the doctor's hand was steady, the rhythm was unhurried, even, deliberate.

"How old are you, son?" Dr. Anderson asked.

"Sixteen."

Dr. Anderson sat without speaking for a moment.

"I'm just trying to remember how I felt and how I thought when I was your age," he said. "My son was off in school at sixteen. You knew him?"

David did not remember Dr. Anderson's son. Mrs. Williams said she had seen him. Before he went off to school he had often ridden with his father when the doctor made his visits. That had been just before the war. Young Dr. Anderson had gone into the army as soon as he graduated from medical school. The transport had been torpedoed while he was going overseas.

"I haven't done all I should," Dr. Anderson went on. "There is so much to do, and most of the people here are backward. They are ignorant and blind. You know I sent my boy away for his high school work. The school here doesn't offer the things a boy should have for medicine. The people think their schools are good enough, but they are not. They don't offer the courses, and the work is poorly done.

I understand they don't give even that much in the colored school."

Mrs. Williams defended the efforts of the teaching staff. They did their best with what they had, but they did not have the facilities. There were not enough teachers.

"I understand, Mrs. Williams," Dr. Anderson said. "The teachers do nobly, yet David is not being prepared for medical school."

"I don't think I could ever feel easy in my mind here," Mrs. Williams said. "But if I could, I still think for our children's sake we should go away."

"Even though I know you folks won't have any more trouble here" — the doctor's fingers folded evenly into a fist — "I think a change might be good. A chance to see some other things. To forget some of the bitterness. Mr. Williams is a fine man. If he leaves, it will be our loss. But he is an excellent mechanic. He can get work anywhere that good men are needed. Why don't you folks move, go up North where David, and Betty Jane too, can have really good schooling? There'll be work in the cities, New York, Detroit, Chicago, or in the smaller places. I guess I wouldn't like the big cities myself. David could go to a good high school and to a state university. I hope he can go on through medical school, keeping in mind that we will be waiting for him when he graduates and completes his internship."

David liked that. Mrs. Williams' face was alight with a new vision, but there were doubts.

"We would have to sell out here," she said. "This was

our home, but perhaps it will never seem the same again. We had plans for improvements and additions."

Dr. Anderson said, "I would be glad to help with the business arrangements."

Mrs. Williams looked at her son. For his future, for the future of David and Betty Jane, no effort would be too great.

"My husband would be the one to say." She hesitated while David held his breath. "I think I would be glad to make the change."

"It will not be easy." The doctor was looking through the window toward the highway that led down and then over the hill toward the town. "It will not be easy. It's not easy for anyone — even for those who have the money they need. It's a long, hard road; but others have made a success of a new life in the North, and I believe you will — and I hope you'll be coming back to South Town. I should like to be here to welcome young Dr. Williams."

15

Two days later Williams insisted on getting up. He shaved himself, and everybody agreed that he looked like a new man. Sitting on the front porch in clean slacks and sport shirt, he enjoyed the sight of passing cars, the friendly waves of those who drove by, and the hearty hand-clasps of those who stopped to wish him well.

"David," he said while Ma was preparing dinner, "your mother tells me that you all are planning to take me away from South Town."

David said they had talked over some plans, but of course everything was up to Pa.

"This is a big decision to make," Pa said. "Lots of our people have left to go North. But I don't know if I'd like it.

Outside of my time in the city, I've never lived any place but here." Ed Williams gazed out the window; his eyes were sort of sad, David thought. "A man doesn't like running away, David. I'm not sure it's the right thing to do. But what I've worried about most of all is your education. And I know you'd have a better chance for a good education somewhere else. New Jersey maybe, or Detroit."

"We got cousins in Detroit," David said. "And the Robertsons live there. Hickey Robertson was here in July. He goes to high school there. He says it's great."

"Yes, we could write some letters," Pa went on. "We've got enough cash to pay off the debt on the place. I wouldn't want to cash in any bonds, but if there wasn't any work right away, the bonds would tide us over for a few months. The only thing is, we'd have to move fast. It's almost time for school to start."

That night Mrs. Williams wrote letters to friends and relatives in Detroit.

The next morning they went in town with David driving. At the bank Pa drew from his savings account and paid the last of the debt on the place. He told Mr. Askew, the bank president, that they were going to sell. Mr. Askew took Mr. and Mrs. Williams into the office and tried to dissuade them from their plans. Nothing was said about the recent trouble, but Mr. Askew did say that conditions would be better, the leading people were going to see to it. Finally he agreed to do everything he could to help find a buyer, and he promised to co-operate in every way. He shook hands with them and said that South Town was very sorry to lose good citizens.

At the post office David stopped the car to mail the letters. When he came out, Mr. Boyd was standing at the gasoline pump across the street in front of the Ford agency. He was dressed in a white linen suit topped by a broad-brimmed Panama hat. He stood and watched the car pull out from the curb. David expected his father to say something, something ugly to give expression to the hate that lay between the two men. Williams said nothing. Boyd made no sign of recognition.

David drove to the corner and swung around the button in a U turn and started back. Now they would pass directly in front of Boyd. David was wishing there was something he could say to show how he felt, something he could do to hurt the man who had hurt his father. As they approached the Ford place, Boyd stepped deliberately from the curb and started slowly across the street. An idea flashed into David's mind. He stepped on the gas, and the car picked up speed.

"No!" It was Pa's voice.

The tires bit into the asphalt as David's foot shifted from accelerator to brake pedal.

Without turning his head, Boyd continued across the street at the same slow pace.

"Let's go home, Son," Pa said softly.

David sat for a moment without moving. His hand trembled as he reached out to shift into low. No one spoke as they rode homeward. From the back seat, Ma put her hand on her son's shoulder, and the trembling went out of his body at the touch. They never spoke afterward of what might have happened.

The news of their plan to leave spread through the county. Few people had telephones, but cars going up and down the highway and along the side roads and down unpaved lanes carried the word.

"The Williamses are moving." "The Williamses are going up North." "Ed Williams is taking his family up to Detroit."

"I don't blame them," they said in the houses.

"If I had a trade, I'd go too," they said at the crossroads stores.

"The Williamses will get along any place," they said in the town and around the countryside, "but we'll miss them. It won't be the same without them in the school, in the church, and everywhere."

On Sunday afternoon the white car of the state police came over the hill. Trooper John Whitlock looked down the highway and saw long rows of cars and mule-drawn wagons and trucks parked at the side of the road. He pushed his foot down on the accelerator, and the car leaped forward. With a blast of the siren, he slipped into the traffic and slammed on the brakes.

"What's the trouble here?" he shouted, leaning from the window. "What's happened?"

"It ain't," an old man said, shaking his head. "It ain't happened, not yet."

The officer got out of the car. He was a large man, wide

in the shoulders and deep in the chest. He unbuckled the flap of his holster.

"What is it, then?" he demanded. "What's going on round here?"

"They going away. Ed Williams's going away," the old man said. "We done come to say good-by."

"All these folks?" Whitlock looked about him. In the yard people were standing. At the door they were going in and out. On the porch were flowers in fruit jars. It was like a wedding, or a funeral. More cars were coming, and some were pulling out. There was nothing here for a policeman to do, unless . . . Whitlock got back into his car and found a place to park.

When Ben Crawford called David to the porch, Trooper Whitlock was directing traffic, waving the curious on and telling tourists that it was just some colored people having a kind of a meeting. They were like that, he said.

Inside the house were more flowers. Some of the friends were crying.

Men, one after the other, took Mr. Williams aside and offered their assistance. They wanted to lend him money, and when he said that it would hardly be necessary, they made him promise that should he be in need of anything, he would write and say so.

Mr. Skipwith and Mr. Brown came together, saying that if he would stay and open a general repair shop, they would help to finance it and see that Williams got all the work he could do. He thanked them but said the education of his children was the most important consideration in his decision to leave.

Mrs. Williams was not prepared for such an ingathering of friends. She had expected a few visitors, and she had prepared some extra pie and cake. Some who came early went back to their homes and returned with more food. They brought fried chicken and ham and more baked goods. Ma was almost ready to change her plans. She had never realized they had so many friends.

Their plan was to leave on Wednesday morning. They would travel by car. They had names and addresses of friends and friends of friends with whom they would be able to stop along the way. Mrs. Williams was not sure she would like the city. Perhaps after they got there, she said, they would go to some smaller place nearby, if Ed found suitable work.

Replies to their letters were coming in. Every letter brought stories of housing shortages in Detroit and news of unemployment, but each said, "Come, come at once." They would have to double up, but there were day beds and sofas and places for them to stay.

On Tuesday Joe Brodnax came in the middle of the morning. He drove up the highway at full speed, and his old coupe leaned far to one side as it turned into the drive.

"Ed, Ed Williams," he cried, jumping from the car and running up the front steps. The whole family had been packing, but they met him at the front door. "Ed, I had a long talk with Mr. Boyd just now. Ed, you got to know. Mr. Boyd's had to give in, Ed."

Joe was so happy he shouted his news. Mr. Boyd had said Joe was to get a raise in pay. He would be paid as much as the white mechanics in the shop. Joe wanted Ed to give up his idea of going away. He wanted Ed to forget all the hard words and the trouble Mr. Boyd had made for him and to come back and get his old job. He was sure the boss would be glad to have him back. Mr. Boyd hadn't exactly said it, but he had asked about Ed. He sure was a changed white man. Seemed like he was sorry about everything, and he wanted to make it up.

"Come on, Ed. For God's sake, come on down there and talk to the man," Joe said. "He told me you was a good worker. He much as said he was sorry you was going away. I know he'd be glad to get you back."

For a moment David wondered. Pa looked at Joe as though he could not believe his words. He sat down in Ma's rocker, and he just kept looking at Joe.

Joe turned to Mrs. Williams and gave more details of what had happened. During the past week people had been calling to see Mr. Boyd. They had gone into the office and talked to him and Mundy. Judge Armstead and the mayor and lots of the other big white folks had been there. For days Mr. Boyd had been really worried; then he called Joe in and told him about his raise.

Ma didn't say anything either. She just listened and nodded sometimes. Then she went over and stood by Pa. She put her hand on his shoulder, and Pa straightened up.

"Thanks, Joe," he said. "Thanks a lot. You been a

good friend to me and my family. I appreciate it, and I'll always remember it."

"But won't you go talk it over, Ed?" Joe was shaking his head with his pleading. "Won't you go talk to the man? I tell you he ain't so high and mighty as he was."

"It wouldn't do no good, Joe." David felt better when he heard Pa's words. "It wouldn't do no good. He's got too much dirt in him for me to go near him. And I got too much hate in me. That night down there I was mad enough to kill him, mad enough to kill anybody whose face was white. I vowed then that if anybody hurt my folks while they had me locked up, I'd kill Boyd and every white person I could before they got me. And while I was there, that man was trying to kill my wife and my children.

"I'm glad to hear what you say about him," Pa went on. "I guess I don't want to kill him really. Maybe some day I'll stop hating him, but I got the feeling that he's the kind of a man that the jailhouse is the kind of a place, a low-down, nasty man that decent folks ain't got no business mixing with. I don't want to talk to him.

"Now you say he's changed. Maybe you're right. I'm glad he's going to treat you like a man, but I got nothing to see him about. They could change the jailhouse too. They could make it into marble and trim it with gold and spread diamonds knee-deep in the alley, but I'd still puke if I went up there. I'd remember. No, Joe. Just tell him you saw me."

When they left, at six o'clock on Wednesday morning, it was like a parade. Israel Crawford, Jr., was standing on the porch with his wife Velvet. They had signed papers to buy the place, and they would move in right away. Furniture, that part of it which Israel or other friends did not buy, was stored in David's room until a home was found up North.

As David got into the car, he heard Josephine bawl out as though she knew her loved ones were going away and leaving her behind.

Pa drove. Betty Jane and David sat on the front seat with him. Ma was in the back with suitcases and boxes and bundles of bedding, things they would need right away, even at the homes of friends.

Behind the Williams car Al Manning came with Mrs. Manning and Elizabeth and Mr. and Mrs. Hutchinson. Ben Crawford drove his father and mother. Brother Dan Jenkins and his family, Mr. Jackson and some of the teachers, Mr. Clayton with Mr. and Mrs. Puryear, the Skipwiths, the Browns, and the Williams family from Centerville.

"Looks like a funeral," David said, trying to make a joke, but no one laughed. It felt like a funeral.

Pa slowed down going by the school. The morning sun was reflected in the windows. The grass had grown high during the summer. David would not be among the older boys who would mow it down with scythes this year.

In the town they turned by the bank. Along Main Street few people walked so early in the morning. Those who saw them waved and called, "God bless you all!"

Beyond the town Pa drove faster. Where the road forked at a grove, he pulled to the side of the highway and stopped.

There were tears and handshakings, hugs and promises to write. Betty Jane wanted to go back.

As the Williams car moved off, Mrs. Manning started singing, and all those with her joined.

God be with you 'til we meet again,
By His counsels guide, uphold you,
With His sheep securely fold you.
God be with you 'til we meet again.

The car wavered in the road as Pa wiped his eyes.